OXFORD WORLD'S CLASSICS

BETWEEN THE ACTS

FRANK KERMODE was King Edward VII Professor of English Literature at Cambridge, and a distinguished scholar and literary critic. His many books include *Romantic Image*, *The Sense of an Ending*, *The Classic*, *The Genesis of Secrecy*, *Forms of Attention*, *History and Value*, *The Art of Reading*, *An Appetite for Poetry*, and *The Uses of Error*. He was also co-editor with John Hollander of *The Oxford Anthology of English Literature*. He was knighted in the New Year's Honours List, 1991. Frank Kermode died in 2010.

OXFORD WORLD'S CLASSICS

For over 100 years Oxford World's Classics have brought readers closer to the world's great literature. Now with over 700 titles—from the 4,000-year-old myths of Mesopotamia to the twentieth century's greatest novels—the series makes available lesser-known as well as celebrated writing.

The pocket-sized hardbacks of the early years contained introductions by Virginia Woolf, T. S. Eliot, Graham Greene, and other literary figures which enriched the experience of reading. Today the series is recognized for its fine scholarship and reliability in texts that span world literature, drama and poetry, religion, philosophy and politics. Each edition includes perceptive commentary and essential background information to meet the changing needs of readers.

OXFORD WORLD'S CLASSICS

VIRGINIA WOOLF

Between the Acts

Edited with an Introduction and Notes by
FRANK KERMODE

OXFORD
UNIVERSITY PRESS

OXFORD

UNIVERSITY PRESS

Great Clarendon Street, Oxford OX2 6DP

Oxford University Press is a department of the University of Oxford.
It furthers the University's objective of excellence in research, scholarship,
and education by publishing worldwide in

Oxford New York

Auckland Bangkok Buenos Aires Cape Town Chennai
Dar es Salaam Delhi Hong Kong Istanbul Karachi Kolkata
Kuala Lumpur Madrid Melbourne Mexico City Mumbai Nairobi
São Paulo Shanghai Taipei Tokyo Toronto

Oxford is a registered trade mark of Oxford University Press
in the UK and in certain other countries

Published in the United States
by Oxford University Press Inc., New York

Editorial material © Frank Kermode 1992
Copyright © David Bradshaw 2000

The moral rights of the author have been asserted

Database right Oxford University Press (maker)

First published as a World's Classics paperback 1992
Reissued as an Oxford World's Classics paperback 1998
Reissued 2008

All rights reserved. No part of this publication may be reproduced,
stored in a retrieval system, or transmitted, in any form or by any means,
without the prior permission in writing of Oxford University Press,
or as expressly permitted by law, or under terms agreed with the appropriate
reprographics rights organizations. Enquiries concerning reproduction
outside the scope of the above should be sent to the Rights Department,
Oxford University Press, at the address above

You must not circulate this book in any other binding or cover
and you must impose this same condition on any acquirer

British Library Cataloguing in Publication Data

Data available

ISBN 978-0-19-953657-3

18

Printed and bound in Great Britain by Clays Ltd, Elcograf S.p.A.

CONTENTS

BIOGRAPHICAL PREFACE

VIRGINIA WOOLF was born Adeline Virginia Stephen on 25 January 1882 at 22 Hyde Park Gate, Kensington. Her father, Leslie Stephen, himself a widower, had married in 1878 Julia Jackson, widow of Herbert Duckworth. Between them they already had four children; a fifth, Vanessa, was born in 1879, a sixth, Thoby, in 1880. There followed Virginia and, in 1883, Adrian.

Both of the parents had strong family associations with literature. Leslie Stephen was the son of Sir James Stephen, a noted historian, and brother of Sir James Fitzjames Stephen, a distinguished lawyer and writer on law. His first wife was a daughter of Thackeray, his second had been an admired associate of the Pre-Raphaelites, and also, like her first husband, had aristocratic connections. Stephen himself is best remembered as the founding editor of the *Dictionary of National Biography*, and as an alpinist, but he was also a remarkable journalist, biographer, and historian of ideas; his *History of English Thought in the Eighteenth Century* (1876) is still of great value. No doubt our strongest idea of him derives from the character of Mr Ramsay in *To the Lighthouse*; for a less impressionistic portrait, which conveys a strong sense of his centrality in the intellectual life of the time, one can consult Noël Annan's *Leslie Stephen* (revised edition, 1984).

Virginia had the free run of her father's library, a better substitute for the public school and university education she was denied than most women of the time could aspire to; her brothers, of course, were sent to Clifton and Westminster. Her mother died in 1895, and in that year she had her first breakdown, possibly related in some way to the sexual molestation of which her half-brother George Duckworth is accused. By 1897 she was able to read again, and did so voraciously: 'Gracious, child, how you gobble,' remarked her father, who, with a liberality and good sense at odds with the age in which they lived, allowed her to choose her reading freely. In other respects her relationship with her father was difficult; his deafness and melancholy, his excessive emotionalism, not helped by successive bereavements, all increased her nervousness.

Stephen fell ill in 1902 and died in 1904. Virginia suffered another breakdown, during which she heard the birds singing in Greek, a language in which she had acquired some competence. On her recovery she moved, with her brothers and sister, to a house in Gordon Square, Bloomsbury; there, and subsequently at several other nearby addresses, what eventually became famous as the Bloomsbury Group took shape.

Virginia had long considered herself a writer. It was in 1905 that she began to write for publication in the *Times Literary Supplement*. In her circle (more loosely drawn than is sometimes supposed) were many whose names are now half-forgotten, but some were or became famous: J. M. Keynes and E. M. Forster and Roger Fry; also Clive Bell, who married Vanessa, Lytton Strachey, who once proposed marriage to her, and Leonard Woolf. Despite much ill health in these years, she travelled a good deal, and had an interesting social life in London. She did a little adult-education teaching, worked for female suffrage, and shared the excitement of Roger Fry's Post-Impressionist Exhibition in 1910. In 1912, after another bout of illness, she married Leonard Woolf.

She was thirty, and had not yet published a book, though *The Voyage Out* was in preparation. It was accepted for publication by her half-brother Gerald Duckworth in 1913 (it appeared in 1915). She was often ill with depression and anorexia, and in 1913 attempted suicide. But after a bout of violent madness her health seemed to settle down, and in 1917 a printing press was installed at Hogarth House, Richmond, where she and her husband were living. The Hogarth Press, later an illustrious institution, but at first meant in part as therapy for Virginia, was now inaugurated. She began *Night and Day*, and finished it in 1918. It was published by Duckworth in 1919, the year in which the Woolfs bought Monk's House, Rodmell, for £700. There, in 1920, she began *Jacob's Room*, finished, and published by the Woolf's own Hogarth Press, in 1922. In the following year she began *Mrs Dalloway* (finished in 1924, published 1925), when she was already working on *To the Lighthouse* (finished and published, after intervals of illness, in 1927). *Orlando*, a fantastic 'biography' of a man—woman, and a tribute to Virginia's close friendship with Vita Sackville-West, was written quite rapidly over the winter of 1927–8, and published, with considerable success, in October. *The Waves* was written and rewritten in 1930 and 1931 (published in October of that year). She had already started on *Flush*, the story of Elizabeth Barrett Browning's pet dog—another success with the public— and in 1932 began work on what became *The Years*.

This brief account of her work during the first twenty years of her marriage is of course incomplete; she had also written and published many shorter works, as well as both series of *The Common Reader*, and *A Room of One's Own*. There have been accounts of the marriage very hostile to Leonard Woolf, but he can hardly be accused of cramping her talent or hindering the development of her career.

Preface

The Years proved an agonizingly difficult book to finish, and was completely rewritten at least twice. Her friend Roger Fry having died in 1934, she planned to write a biography, but illnesses in 1936 delayed the project; towards the end of that year she began instead the polemical *Three Guineas*, published in 1938. *The Years* had meanwhile appeared in 1937, by which time she was again at work on the Fry biography, and already sketching in her head the book that was to be *Between the Acts*. *Roger Fry* was published in the terrifying summer of 1940. By the autumn of that year many of the familiar Bloomsbury houses had been destroyed or badly damaged by bombs. Back at Monk's House, she worked on *Between the Acts*, and finished it in February 1941. Thereafter her mental condition deteriorated alarmingly, and on 28 March, unable to face another bout of insanity, she drowned herself in the River Ouse.

Her career as a writer of fiction covers the years 1912–41, thirty years distracted by intermittent serious illness as well as by the demands, which she regarded as very important, of family and friends, and by the need or desire to write literary criticism and social comment. Her industry was extraordinary—nine highly-wrought novels, two or three of them among the great masterpieces of the form in this century, along with all the other writings, including the copious journals and letters that have been edited and published in recent years. Firmly set though her life was in the 'Bloomsbury' context—the agnostic ethic transformed from that of her forebears, the influence of G. E. Moore and the Cambridge Apostles, the individual brilliance of J. M. Keynes, Strachey, Forster, and the others—we have come more and more to value the distinctiveness of her talent, so that she seems more and more to stand free of any context that might be thought to limit her. None of that company—except, perhaps, T. S. Eliot, who was on the fringe of it—did more to establish the possibilities of literary innovation, or to demonstrate that such innovation must be brought about by minds familiar with the innovations of the past. This is true originality. It was Eliot who said of *Jacob's Room* that in that book she had freed herself from any compromise between the traditional novel and her original gift; it was the freedom he himself sought in *The Waste Land*, published in the same year, a freedom that was dependent upon one's knowing with intimacy that with which compromise must be avoided, so that the knowledge became part of the originality. In fact she had 'gobbled' her father's books to a higher purpose than he could have understood.

INTRODUCTION

IN 1937 Virginia Woolf published *The Years*, the product
of half a decade of laborious composition and revision. The
work had been uncongenial, though in the course of it she
once remarked that, looming behind *The Years*, she could
'just see the shape of pure poetry beckoning me'. Postpon-
ing attention to that vision, she began work on the feminist
polemic *Three Guineas*, which she finished in January
1938. When her friend Roger Fry died in 1934, she had
undertaken to write his biography; but that work, like
everything else, was interrupted by a breakdown in the
summer of 1936, and she did not begin it in earnest until
April 1938. By that time she had lost her enthusiasm for
the task, and turned for relief towards that 'beckoning
shape', which now took more distinct form as a story
called *Pointz Hall*.

The first intimation of the nature of this new enterprise
had occurred in January 1938:

Will another novel ever swim up? ... The only hint I have
towards it is that it's to be dialogue: and poetry: and prose; all
quite distinct. No more long closely written books [like *The
Years*]. But I have no impulse; and shall wait; and shan't mind if
the impulse never formulates; though I suspect one of these days
I shall get that old rapture.

At the moment when she was starting serious work on
the Fry biography, she was also predicting that *Pointz Hall*
would be 'a book about England and English literature'.
And on 12 April 1938 she 'began making up again:
Summers night: a complete whole: that's my idea'. She was
apprehensive as well as rapturous: 'here I am sketching out

a new book; only dont please impose that huge burden on me again, I implore. Let it be random & tentative . . . dont, I implore, lay down a scheme; call in all the cosmic immensities; & force my tired & diffident brain to embrace another whole . . . ' (*Diary*, 26 April 1938). She worked at the novel off and on through 1939, and, with more concentration, from May 1940. Now renamed *Between the Acts*, it was finished on 23 November 1940.

'Never', says her biographer Quentin Bell, 'had a novel of hers flowed so rapidly, so effortlessly, from her pen; there were no checks, doubts, despairs, struggles or revisions'. But 'the ending of a novel was always a period of danger for her'. Assailed by doubts, she wrote to John Lehmann at the Hogarth Press (24 March 1941) to say she did not want the book to be published in its present form; they should delay publication, now imminent, until the autumn, and she would meanwhile revise it. When her husband Leonard posted this letter he added a note of his own, telling Lehmann that Virginia was on the verge of a mental breakdown. Four days later she drowned herself in the Ouse. *Between the Acts* was published that spring, with a note by Leonard explaining that it had not had the author's final revisions.

Between the Acts was for the most part written in a desperate time, when France had fallen and Britain was under heavy attack from the air. The Woolfs had expected the war, which for the Western allies began quietly, to flare up at this moment: 'oh, it's a queer sense of suspense,' wrote Woolf in her diary in February, 'being led up to the spring of 1940.' Four months later the whole of Western Europe was lost. As a Jewish intellectual, Leonard Woolf had a clear idea of what he could expect should the Germans occupy Britain. From their country house near the south coast they watched some of the air battles that began the defence, took shelter from bombs, and discussed the desirability of suicide. When the German air assault switched to London, their Bloomsbury house was damaged; another for which they still paid rent was totally destroyed, and so was the house of Virginia's sister, Vanessa Bell.

This was a war it hardly seemed possible to win; and in any case it all too clearly represented some kind of ending—to a way of life at least, and perhaps to a whole civilization. A book that was being written during the Dunkirk evacuation of May 1940, the Battle of Britain that followed in the autumn, and then the London blitz of the winter of 1940 might be expected to concern itself with such endings, as well as with intimations of endings more personal. On 27 June 1940—after the French capitulation—Woolf wrote that she could not conceive 'that there will be a 27th June, 1941'. Perhaps she was at the same time looking back a year to June 1939, which is where she placed the day's events of *Between the Acts*. That summer before the war might be taken as a true moment of crisis: Barcelona had fallen to Franco, Austria and Czechoslovakia had been swallowed by the future enemy, and Poland was under immediate and fatal threat. There was no question of another compromise or surrender like the Munich Agreement of September 1938. These were unmistakably the last moments of the old world.

It is no cause for wonder that *Between the Acts*, with its peculiarities of style and structure, its privacies and inwardnesses, was not very fully appreciated in 1941 or in the war years that followed; people were desperately busy, or simply desperate. Now, almost half a century later, when there is more leisure and more desire to come to terms with the book, to say nothing of the impetus provided by the new feminism, there are different impediments: much that might have seemed obvious in the 1940s has become considerably less so. Thus we are told by one well-esteemed Woolf scholar that the book is 'set near Roman ruins in wartime Britain'; I suppose it is possible to think of Roman roads as ruins, but it is not easy to see how an attentive reader could even now suppose that on the day of the story the war has already begun. Not to see that the book is deliberately placed on the threshold between peace and war, between a known past and an unknown but probably appalling future, is to miss what used to be the most obvious thing about it.

All manner of irrelevant fancies pour into the vacuum created by this basic failure of understanding. For instance, the same author maintains that Isa Oliver, on the strength of her O'Neil aunts, represents the oppressed Irish as well as the oppressed sex; that Mrs Manresa is named, not, as seems more likely, after a well-known Chelsea street, but after the place where St Ignatius wrote his *Spiritual Exercises*; that, since a nightingale is mentioned, and since the book contains a great many swallows, the plot must be based on the myth of Procne and Philomela, described as another 'war story'; and, finally, that the novel exhibits 'a classical Marxist dialectic' . . .

England, and more particularly the England of 1939, has evidently become a remote and misty scene. This is doubtless in part due to the usual action of time, though something must be attributed to careless, partisan, and licentious interpretation. It is probably useless to complain. The book may still reveal its qualities to readers more soberly attentive not only to the historical context but also to the text.

*

Introduction

The kind of book Woolf always wanted to write—'a complete whole'—was also the kind which placed on her that 'huge burden'. In the modernist manner she consciously aspired to a *summa*, a novel in which would be written everything susceptible to her manner of writing. That she could have thought of *Between the Acts* as coming close to that achievement may surprise us; or 'random and tentative', in manner more like *Orlando* than *The Waves* or *To the Lighthouse*, or those other works which, each in its own way, attempt to get all or a great deal of a particular world into a book. Yet she herself called *Between the Acts* 'more quintessential than the others'. And that is a claim not to be casually dismissed.

The reconciliation of fantasy and randomness with wholeness was long a preoccupation of this author.

Now is life very solid or very shifting? I am haunted by the two contradictions. This has gone on for ever: will last for ever; goes down to the bottom of the world—this moment I stand on. Also it is transitory, flying, diaphanous ... Perhaps it may be that though we change; one flying after another, so quick so quick, yet we are somehow successive, & continuous—we human beings; & show the light through.

This passage from the diary, written in January 1929, offers one version of the antithesis— 'solid is it, or shifting?'—which seems always to dominate her imagination.

From time to time the usual means by which writers try to impose coherence and unity on the scattered and transitory are dismissed by Woolf as inadequate or obsolete. One such means was plot. 'Don't bother about the plot,' we are told. 'The plot's nothing.' As Bernard had said in *The Waves*: 'Life is not susceptible to the treatment we give it when we try to tell it.' Indeed Bernard the writer, the story-teller, repeatedly inveighs against stories. 'How tired I am of stories ... I begin to long for some little language such as lovers use, broken words, inarticulate words, like the shuffling of feet upon the pavement.'

Here is a hint as to the nature of that 'poem', *Between the Acts*—so unlike *The Years*, so 'random and tentative', yet somehow claiming to be a complete whole. It must be something that combines unity and dispersity by the action of a special 'little language'. The world will be present in the texture of the book itself, not in reference to 'cosmic intensities'. The special little language may be infantile, like the little language of lovers, or unintelligible, like that of the street-singer outside Regent's Park tube station in *Mrs Dalloway* or that of the nameless children of the caretaker, who, at the end of *The Years*, baffle the adults with their nonsense song in a language vaguely resembling Greek (the language the birds spoke to Woolf in her madness, and to Septimus in *Mrs Dalloway*). Are these children merely ignorant, as members of 'the younger generation' of the proletariat tend to be? Is their performance beautiful or hideous? The grown-ups cannot say; they understand not a word of it. But theirs is a little language approximating the little language appropriate to art.

The little language of *Between the Acts*, the dialect which expresses, indeed which *is*, its world, is not a mock-Greek, and it makes ordinary sense if that is what readers are looking for; but, if they look for more, yet do not seek it in the texture, their quest for profundity may drive them away from the language and even tempt them to invent secret mythologies, occult allusions to Ignatius of Loyola and Procne and Philomel. The more sceptical may dismiss the book as a somewhat bewildering trifle which, like the pageant it contains, probably gave more pleasure, not to speak of 'glory', to the author than to her audience.

The little language did not come full-formed into being; it had its antecedents. But now, given its fullest expression in the last novel, it subordinates to its own purposes, and to an unprecedented degree, all apparently veracious reports on the random world. This is really another way of talking about the process Woolf, in her essay 'Mr Bennett and Mrs Brown', called 'referring each word to my vision'. Elsewhere she described her task thus: to cut away all superfluity and 'give the moment whole . . . Say that the moment is a combination of thought; sensation; the voice of the sea.' At the time she was working on *The Waves*. It was a task to be performed only by the act of writing: 'nothing makes a whole', she remarked in 1933, 'except when I am writing'.

Wholeness, as Bernard saw and as *Between the Acts* tries to demonstrate, is something imposed on or discovered in the world by writing. And the wholeness would be false without the randomness. To make a fuss about everything, it may be necessary, at least in appearance, to make a 'fuss about nothing'. To produce your *summa* you may need to submit reality, whatever that is thought to be—'cancer and calico' she once called it—to language, to the inward-looking fuss of language, to what looks like linguistic self-indulgence and might even, at moments, resemble a little the manner of the later Joyce.

'It's very unsettled [remarks Mrs Swithin]. It'll rain, I'm afraid. We can only pray,' she added, and fingered her crucifix. 'And provide umbrellas,' said her brother. Lucy flushed. He had struck her faith. When she said 'pray', he added 'umbrellas'. She half covered the cross with her fingers. She shrank; she cowered; but

next moment she exclaimed: 'Oh there they are—the darlings!'
The perambulator was passing across the lawn. (p. 22)

It is correct to say that this conversation deals with a
conflict between faith and practical reason which often
recurs in the relationship of sister and brother, old Lucy
and old Bart. But it may be more to the point to notice
that, from the merger of 'umbrellas' and 'prayer', you can
roughly derive 'perambulators', and the perambulator,
after thoughtful preparation many pages earlier, enters on
cue; something in the world obeys the summons of an
unconstrained and imperious little language. Round this
word 'perambulator' the narrative arranges itself in a
semblance of tidiness; first the talk of the weather, then
Mrs Swithin's remarks about the health of the little boy.
But the portmanteau word, reconciling opposites, is itself
generated not by narrative but by language—and not
merely by this particular bit of language.

'If it's fine . . . if it's wet; wet will it be or fine?' is a
persistent rhythm, and that rhythm is even responsible for
Mrs Swithin's name; St Swithin's day (15 July) is supposed
to determine whether it will be wet or fine for the next
forty days. ' "The Swithins", Mrs Swithin began. Then she
stopped. Bart would crack another joke about Saints, if she
gave him the chance. And she had had two jokes cracked
at her already; one about an umbrella, another about
superstition' (p. 28).

There is indeed much talk about the weather, justified
by worries about the afternoon's entertainment, which will
be out of doors if it is fine, in the barn if it is wet. The
matter seems trivial enough, though to a reader familiar
with earlier books of Woolf it may have a certain reso-
nance; *To the Lighthouse* begins with Mrs Ramsay's promise

that James will at last go to the lighthouse tomorrow, 'if it's fine'. His father, happy with the chance to disillusion his son and ridicule his wife, now says firmly, 'But . . . it won't be fine,' and congratulates himself on always speaking the truth, however disagreeable; Mrs Ramsay, however, still says 'But it may be fine—I expect it will be fine.' However, at the end of the first section she says 'It's going to be wet tomorrow,' simply to express her love, and triumph in it. Indeed the question, wet will it be or fine? echoes through that book also, a rhythm affirming its importance by its intermittent presence, very much part of its wholeness, which is like Mrs Ramsay's day as she suddenly feels it to have been:

All the odds and ends of the day stuck to this magnet [a line of poetry casually read a moment before]; her mind felt swept, felt clean. And then there it was, suddenly entire; she held it in her hands, beautiful and reasonable, clear and complete, the essence sucked out of life and held rounded here—the sonnet.

However, we do not need to attribute to such echoes the total effect of all the alternatives or antitheses, trivial in themselves, which are the very texture of *Between the Acts*—a house in a hollow that might have been on a hill, a woman sitting in the garden discussing cesspools, and explaining that she fears not cows but horses; who comes from an old Cornish family but now lives further to the north, where, as she surely ought to understand, the bird she hears cannot be a nightingale, must be a daylight bird, since nightingales do not come so far north. These random oppositions occur on the first page of the novel. They recur with unmistakable and apparently pointless insistence: one red cow moves forward, the other stands still; some rose, others stooped; one child had been chosen, another not;

the horse had gone, but the cow remained; there are those
who have been to Greece, and those who have never been
to Greece; and so forth. These are antithetical views as it
were imposed on the solid or shifting world. That one
child is chosen already implies the existence of others who
are not; the total of those who have been to Greece and
those who have not is the entire population.

In the same way there are opposed views about matters
one might have thought easily settled: where, for example,
is Poyntz Hall? 'They were so far from the sea. A hundred
miles away, Mrs Swithin said; no, perhaps a hundred and
fifty . . . Are we really . . . a hundred miles from the sea?
"Thirty-five only," her father-in-law said, as if he had
whipped out a tape-measure from his pocket and measured
it exactly' (p. 27). We are invited, though without any
irritable reaching after fact and reason, to attend to this
mixture of absurd vagueness and improbable exactness. (In
any case, nowhere in Britain can be a hundred and fifty, or
perhaps even a hundred, miles from the sea.) It is natural
to suppose that these strange alternatives are mere echoes
of apparently more significant antitheses—peace and war,
men and women, past and present, present and future,
unity and dispersity—that they represent a sort of dither-
ing at the dividing line between opposites, or a dwelling on
the haloes of imprecision that at significant moments—
when we match imagination with the world—hover round
our perceptions. But what, in the first instance, they
affirm is that the making of complete wholes must depend
on the dispersions and fortuities of the private, the little
language.

That language has its characteristic rhythms—not only
the wet-or-fine seesawing, but a triadic pattern that has a
long history in Woolf, and has already appeared in this

Introduction: 'she shrank, she cowered . . . she exclaimed . . .'; 'thought; sensation; the voice of the sea'. 'This has gone on for ever; will last for ever; goes down to the bottom of the world . . . Also it is transitory, flying, diaphanous.' The triad is often highlighted by the proximity of a monad or a dyad, as in *Mrs Dalloway*. 'In people's eyes; in the swing, tramp, and trudge; in the bellow and the uproar . . . in the triumph and the jingle and the strange high singing [triad within triad] of some aeroplane overhead was what she loved; life; London; this moment of June.'

The punctuation is nearly always, as it is here, inescapably heavy; it lightens only when the elements of the triad become more expansive, and when what is needed is an impression of pace or exhilaration: 'a beating, a stirring of galloping ponies, tapping of cricket bats'. Or a characteristic inversion can throw the triad into higher relief: 'Cold, heartless, a prude he called her'; or in the sky-sign, 'A C was it? an E, then an L?' Things of this sort occur on almost every page of the book.

They also help to give *The Waves* some of its characteristic rhythms: 'Toast and butter, coffee and bacon, *The Times* and letters . . .';

The clock ticks; the woman sneezes; the waiter comes—there is a gradual coming together, running into one, acceleration and unification. Listen: a whistle sounds, wheels rush, the door creaks on its hinges. I regain the sense of the complexity and the reality and the struggle, for which I thank you. And with some pity, some envy, and much good will, take your hand and bid you goodnight.

Bernard may not have the little language he needs, but his meditations foreshadow its patterns:

Introduction

I need a little language such as lovers use, words of one syllable
such as children speak when they come into the room and find
their mother sewing and pick up some scrap of bright wool, a
feather, or a shred of chintz. I need a howl, a cry . . . Nothing
neat. Nothing that comes down with all its feet on the floor.
None of those resonances and lovely echoes that break and chime
from nerve to nerve in our breasts, making wild music, false
phrases. I have done with phrases.

He ends with triads: 'I must haul myself up, and find
the particular coat that belongs to me; must push my arms
into the sleeves, must muffle myself against the night air
and be off. I, I, I, tired as I am, spent as I am, and almost
worn out . . .' He has given up story and plot, and he has
given up wild music, false phrases, and lovely echoes in
favour of random scraps and cries and words of one
syllable; but he keeps time, sets his own seal on the little
language, as Woolf herself did: 'summer's night: a complete
whole: that's my idea'.

The secret of the texture may well be that there are scraps
that will remain merely scraps except by association with
others more obviously significant, related to them by
rhythm and perhaps by resemblances of structure, which
refer to the integrity of the book and possibly of the world
perceived in 'rapture'. Sometimes this is achieved by an
original narrative device, to understand which one might
look at the apparently intrusive story of the girl raped by
guardsmen. Isa reads it in the old man's newspaper, which
has already been used to terrify little George. The girl,
resisting a trooper, is said to have hit him about the face.
Isa visualizes the scene, whereupon Mrs Swithin enters
with a hammer she has borrowed to nail a placard on the
barn. She and her brother turn once again to the question,

'which will it be? . . . Wet or fine?' Isa has heard this discussion every summer for seven years. 'Every year they said, would it be wet or fine; and every year it was—one or the other. The same chime followed the same chime, only this year beneath the chime she heard: "The girl screamed and hit him about the face with a hammer"' (p. 20).

Here we are directly offered the possibility of giving a special sense to the reiterated paradox, as if a tone has been added to the niggling little figure 'wet or fine', giving it a new coloration, a quality of the minor; setting 'this year' apart by transforming the perennial antithesis. But the boldness of the passage lies in the conflation of the girl's resistance and Mrs Swithin's hammer, innocently stolen, innocently used, though drawn now into a moment of horrible defensive violence, so that the pageant (in the barn if wet) and certain aspects of Mrs Swithin (her wet-or-fine name, her weak struggle with her antithetical but complementary brother, her interest in the violent prehistory of the world, the cross which, for her, makes possible a union of that world with another 'immensity') are transferred to the scene of soldierly lust and the screams of a victim under the imminence of war.

This is work for the reader, and the demands on the reader are almost exorbitant. Let me return, in this connection, to the matter of antithesis as mere rhythm, and antithesis as possibly more resonant than such a description suggests. Isa wonders whether the fish will be fresh or not; Mrs Swithin has to decide whether to winter at Kensington or Kew (she does neither, wintering in a third resort). There is what I have read, and what I have not read. There is pressing ahead and standing still, retreating and advancing, sitting and standing, falling and repairing; notices nailed up and torn down; sandwiches some neat, some not (one cuts the bread, the other the ham); there are flowers that flash and fade; there are simples and gentry; there is following and staying, inside and outside, talk and silence, night and day, sunlight and moonlight, being awake and being asleep, summer and winter. There are some and there are others; some acting hastily, some guiltily; some old and some in the prime of life. There is past and present, joy and suffering, birth and death, love and hate.

The continuous stream of such locutions seems to suggest antithesis as a principle of this world, as if one could arrange this world in two columns, one headed *un-*, or unity, and the other *dis-*, or dispersity, and thus account for the whole, by a gesture like that which amalgamates 'prayer' and 'umbrellas'. If you put together the pageants when it rained, and the pageants when it was fine, you have all the pageants and all the days together; wet and fine may be reconciled by prayer and umbrellas. All the antitheses resemble one another, and that is what the world is like, in the large as well as the small.

'Retreating and advancing', for example. That this expression entails more than the movement of cows or swallows may be inferred from William Dodge's remark to Isa: '"The doom of sudden death hanging over us ... There's no retreating or advancing"—he was thinking of the old lady showing him the house—"for us as for them"' (p. 103). 'The future shadowed their present, like the sun coming through the many-veined transparent vine leaf; a criss-cross of lines making no pattern' (p. 103). The antitheses are that absence of pattern and also the pattern: present and future, birth and death, love and hate, prayer and umbrellas, the portraits of man and woman, each leading in a different direction, one to talk, one to silence, which together make up the unending conversation of the world.

Introduction

The antitheses are fantasticated, forced on our attention by another device, a mannered inversion—a habit of Woolf's, as in 'Solid is it or shifting?' 'Intentional was it or accidental?' 'Wet will it be or fine?' 'Snobs they were'; 'pearls they were'; 'Utterly impossible was it?' 'malversation of trusts, was it?' 'Vulgar she was . . .'; 'Happy he was as a boy.' And they are counterpointed against that other pattern, that other set of criss-crosses that show through the text: the triads, the threefold ply: orts, scraps, and fragments; this, that, and the other; she rose, she paused, she offered her hand; Bart's mother was very stout, kept her tea-caddy locked, gave him a copy of Byron in that very room. There was a butler, a lady's maid, and a Waterloo bullet; a cook, a costume, and a feller; flowing fields, heath, and woods; a room empty, empty, empty, silent, silent, silent; a triple mirror and three faces of Isa; a perambulator, two nurses, and the little boy George; a tingling, tangling, vibrating like that of a propeller—'faster, faster, faster, it whizzed, whirred, buzzed . . .'. These are casual collocations of these two principles, pinned into the narrative.

Note, for example, the combinations of antithesis and triad throughout this passage:

At this early hour of a June morning the library was empty. Mrs Giles had to visit the kitchen. Mr Oliver still tramped the terrace. And Mrs Swithin was of course at church. The light but variable breeze, foretold by the weather expert, flapped the yellow curtain, tossing light, then shadow. The fire greyed, then glowed, and the tortoiseshell butterfly beat on the lower pane of the window; beat, beat, beat; repeating that if no human being ever came, never, never, never, the books would be mouldy, the fire out and the tortoiseshell butterfly dead on the pane. (pp. 15–16).

Introduction

Here are principles of organization, the chemical bonds of a world that are exposed in grosser form in such triads as past, present, and future; love, hate and violence; and in such doublets as town and country, man and woman; though these can become triadic, as when Dodge's sexual nature is interposed between those of Isa and Giles, or Mrs Manresa throws her urban being into the pleasures of rusticity, offering herself as a third term between town and country.

In such a world there are wanton interactions between the parts of language that constitute it. They are here manifest in rhyme. Rhyme, as W. K. Wimsatt once wrote, imposes 'upon the logical pattern of expressed argument a kind of fixative counterpattern of alogical implication'.[1] Mrs Oliver's rhyming is not of the sort that causes surprising distortions or interruptions of the plain sense; she tends to the obvious, as in this passage, arising out of association with the airplane propeller at Croydon:

'Where we know not, where we go not, neither know nor care,' she hummed. 'Flying, rushing through the ambient, incandescent, summer silent . . .'

The rhyme was 'air'. She put down her brush. She took up the telephone. (p. 14)

To rhyme the monosyllabic verbs 'know' and 'go', and the monosyllabic nouns 'care' and 'air', would hardly impress a Wimsatt as the formation of a valuable counterpattern of the kind he describes in Pope, but the object is otherwise: daydreaming ease, lack of resistance; or we find her silently addressing the visitor in the rhythm of a child's verse: 'O[r] what are your rings for, and your nails, and

[1] W. K. Wimsatt, 'One Relation of Rhyme to Reason', in his *The Verbal Icon* Lexington: University of Kentucky Press, (1954), 153–66.

that really adorable little straw hat?' (p. 36). Isa's normal rhythms are hazy, romantic ('To what dark antre of the unvisited earth,' etc.). The verses that come to her mind at need are from Keats's 'To the Nightingale'—she and William Dodge between them manage an inaccurate rendering of three lines, forming an alliance or union of sorts, symbolized also by the coffee-cup, knocked over by Isa, caught and lovingly appraised by Dodge; a sort of narrative rhyme. The resistances are to be sought elsewhere, in other kinds of rhyme: the prayer and the umbrella, the hammer and the girl.

Nevertheless rhythms and rhymes escape from Isa's daydreams and become more criss-crosses in the text: Mrs Manresa arrives, a rock 'raced round, embraced'. She talks in a hearty, thumping rhythm: 'A seat at the table—that's all we want. We have our grub. We have our glasses' (p. 35). The absurd military march of Giles after he kills the snake has its own imposed rhythm: 'But it was action. Action relieved him. He strode to the Barn, with blood on his shoes' (p. 89). His progress towards his goal had been marked with a different rhythm, perhaps to simulate his childish stone-kicking. What he actually achieves is to crush an unbearable antithesis, a kind of emblem, even a kind of rhyme, symbol of a rapacity that achieves not its end but mere horror: 'The snake was unable to swallow; the toad was unable to die' (p. 89). Like Giles, the horribly ill-assorted pair—antithetical, incompatible, but united— is given its own deliberate rhythm.

The swallows have their own rhythm also; their 'darting seemed, by the regularity of the trees, to make a pattern, dancing, like the Russians, only not to music, but to the unheard rhythm of their own wild hearts' (pp. 59–60). Inside the barn the swallows complicate the texture by rhyme and assonance, playing against the summons to follow, against the yellow of the banner and the yellow of the cake on the plate. Mrs Swithin remarks that the swallows come every year, a perpetual temporal rhythm—a fancy characteristically doubted by the patient, patronizing Mrs Manresa. Isa rhymes 'turn away' and 'array' before sliding off into another easy rhythmic fantasy; but she reminds us of the main poem of the barn when she mentions the yellow woodpecker and observes the yellow festoons left over from the Coronation. Bart more than once remembers Swinburne's 'Swallow, my sister, O sister swallow', though without getting on to the third line: 'A thousand summers are over and dead . . .' And he reflects that his sister 'belonged to the unifiers; he to the separatists'. It is true of the old lady; she is intimately connected, metaphorically rhymes with, the swallow ('she perched on the edge of a chair like a bird on a telegraph wire before starting for Africa'), as the swallow roughly rhymes with 'yellow' and 'follow'; 'follow' is itself associated, as in a different kind of rhyme, with the word 'dispersed'.

These rhymes and rhythms also infect the language of the audience, even of old Cobbet ('What was in her mind, eh? What idea lay behind, eh? What made her endue the antique with this glamour—this sham lure . . . ?), (p. 87)). 'Isa' is even made to rhyme with 'Manresa'. Antithetical to reason, rhyme words are attracted by each other and also repelled; they do a certain violence. They can therefore be figures of human relationships, Mrs Swithin and her brother, Isa and her husband, Isa and Dodge, Giles and Mrs Manresa. Mrs Manresa, mockingly compared to the Belle Dame sans Merci and to the Venus of *Phèdre*, 'tout entière à sa proie attachée', bridges two worlds like a rhyme—the world of new vulgar wealth, perhaps, and the world of the Olivers; Giles, changing from city to cricket clothes, is another such bridge. The book is full of them, Wells's *History* bridging the Piccadilly of rhododendron forest and mastodon with the present moment, the maid entering, half-maid and half-monster; *The Times*, with its news of the crisis in France, converting the old man's head into a monster to frighten the child. In the final tableau the antitheses of No and Yes, present and past, love and hate, are restated in a coda set 'in the heart of darkness', an expression not used without connotations of horror at the implications of human—indeed sexual—action and interaction.

The pageant, of course, is the main contrapuntal instrument. It is a self-deprecating view of the place of art in the world, a huge patch on the texture of the book, an alogical rhyme. People in the story, as well as the reader, wonder what it means. As an attempt to make a whole of the orts, scraps, and fragments, a costly attempt for Miss La Trobe ('that huge burden'), it hardly seems to represent a success. Since it is, in a sense, what is called a *mise-en-abyme* of the book that frames it, reflecting the labour and the rapture of Virginia Woolf's own composition, we may take it that when it is ineffective it is intended to be so; that its scrappy view of the past, its parodies, its rhymes, are part of a process that ends at once in rapture and in failure.

'Here are the poets from whom we descend by way of the mind,' says Lucy to William Dodge in the library. And here they are again, in Miss La Trobe's pageant, foregrounded against the chuff and tick of the gramophone that signifies passing time, and the silences, intended and not intended, that interrupt human transactions with time. Here, too, are the accidents that can occur in its course, like the shower or the lowing of the cattle, seized upon as graces beyond the reach of art, as the happy though momentary transcendence of the antitheses of normal time and the time of the epiphany, of art and nature, of actor and audience.

There is enough history in the pageant to justify the background chorus of peasants, on whose labour it is all founded, and enough emphasis on the tawdriness of costume and performance to convince us that this is a cheap modern version of the past; queens and policemen eminent, dominant, supported by music blatant, elatant—it is a joke, as well as a past. In the Elizabethan section there is a play within the pageant that is within the novel; it is not much, but it is enough to remind Isa of the third element in the threefold ply, which is made up of Love, Hate, and Peace. The hereditary village idiot, in and out of the play, also crosses the frontier between audience and players, and between past and present. The ancient lady, arthritic, indigenous, joins the play by her cackle of laughter, as Manresa does by her loud performance of applause.

Miss La Trobe, like all narrative artists, however skimble-skamble, has to fight a battle against time, which must not be permitted to spill the brewed emotion. With the Interval, however, time defeats her; 'dispersed are we'—the unity of play and audience is destroyed. 'High and dry', murmurs Isa. 'Broken is the threefold ply.' Miss La Trobe takes comfort in the Conradian thought that she may for a moment have 'made them see': 'A vision imparted was relief from agony.' But the moment is over; dispersed, they follow one another, no longer to see but to take tea.

After tea she renews the struggle against time, in which her best ally is music. She provides a bit of Restoration comedy, and an admirable pastiche of Collins, which, with the music and the view make 'a triple melody', and that gives some content to the audience; but again illusion fails. 'This is death . . . death.' But there is also grace, and the cows fill the meaningless gap: 'Thank heaven!' says La Trobe. When Mrs Swithin congratulates her—she might she says, inflamed by a glimpse of glory, have herself played Cleopatra—the author is again for a moment possessed by glory. But she must now turn once more to the preservation of the illusion of art. Across the Victorian scene fly swallows, lacing it to the main plot. Mrs Swithin best understands what is happening, though she is unable to explain it: with the help of her cross she can grasp 'one-making'. The others cannot. So deprived, Isa, William, and Giles converse in a silent dialogue of unhappiness.

But the main act of unification is still to come. Miss La Trobe will 'douche' the audience in present time—swallows, cows, the tick of the needle—and then, as the pageant reaches the present day, turn the actors into walking mirrors, so that the audience becomes what it sees, chiming or rhyming with their own unexpected images. At first the pause goes wrong ('death, death, death . . . when the illusion fails') but then the artist is vouchsafed another grace, the shower that arrives out of the blue and saves her again. Her symbolic scenery (civilization in ruins, being rebuilt, etc.—the Great War) becomes in its turn the setting for swallows, retreating and advancing; for cows lowing; for a jerky modern dance. Then 'the looking glasses darted, flashed, exposed' the audience, now themselves the players: play and audience, audience and image, for a moment rhyme. Only Mrs Manresa is coarsely equal to this moment, using one of the looking-glasses to freshen her make-up. Then comes a bodiless voice, condemning, contemptuous of the mirrored throng; but music also comes, a unity of oppositions. The parson sums up, benignly and not stupidly; the orts, scraps, and fragments of the world, which they have seen themselves representing, *should* unite. But unification is merely a pious hope, not an opportunity; and his word, 'opportunity', is cut in half by a flight of military aircraft.

When it is all over Miss La Trobe is not there to be thanked; the machine chuffs again, and then plays '*God* . . . (they all rose to their feet) *Save the King*', the title cut in half to echo the injury to 'opportunity'. 'If one spirit animates the whole,' somebody says helpfully, 'what about the aeroplanes?' Others speculate about conditions in Europe, or discuss aspects of the play. They have had an inkling of unity but are now dispersing, dispersed. Only Lucy, standing at the pool as the housemaid had done during lunch, sees in the variegated fish a vision of 'beauty, power and glory in ourselves'. The antithetical complement of that triadic vision or illusion, she knows, is her brother's rationality.

It is to Miss La Trobe in solitude that glory comes once more, followed by the pain of failure, which is followed, in a rhythm of creativeness, by the rapturous epiphany of the starlings attacking the tree, syllabling life, a moment's plenitude, a whole made of dispersed parts. Even as old Mrs Chalmers passes on her way to the cemetery, the germ of the new work manifests itself, the new poem of unity won from dispersity in a momentary glory. She hears 'words without meaning—wonderful words', a new access of the necessary little language; and her nascent vision melts into the dark union of Giles and Isa, disparate and contentious parts about to come together, as if La Trobe were creating the wordless scene with which the book ends.

Introduction

It is curious that the relation of the framing story and the framed pageant is the reverse of what one might expect: the experience of creation is represented in the La Trobe story; the finished work, the tree pelted with starlings, is in the story of the Olivers, set at the crisis, in that summer when we did not know certainly if the political weather of Europe would be wet or fine; or rather we did know, but were caught as if in a still moment of history—like, perhaps, that long moment in *Macbeth* when, his mind still not quite made up, Macbeth is challenged by his wife to be a man and murder. *Between the Acts* is the poem of that other crisis, and for its author as for Miss La Trobe it was the agent of both glory and death.

NOTE ON THE TEXT

THE present text is that of the first English edition, published in July 1941, with two emendations, few insignificant changes of punctuation, and four slight alterations taken from the first American edition of the same month. These are as follows:

- [21.6] The words 'one moment', lacking in the copytext, have been supplied.
- [30.25] Sands for sand
- [80.9] lorgnette *for* lorgnettes
- [85] The dialogue of the pageant being as a rule in italic, the reading of the English edition ('A-maying, a-maying,' they bawled. 'In and out and round about, a-maying, a-maying . . .') has been regularized.
- [117] *it's her heart* for *its her heart*
- [167.8] megaphonic *for* megaphontic

The text of the first edition is, evidently, a 'clean' one. Leonard Woolf prefixed the following note to that edition:

> The MS. of this book had been completed, but had not been finally revised for the printer, at the time of Virginia Woolf's death. She would not, I believe, have made any large or material alterations in it, though she would probably have made a good many small corrections or revisions before passing the final proofs.
>
> LEONARD WOOLF

This edition makes minor adjustments to hyphenation, word division ('tomorrow', 'tonight', 'someone', etc.), 'ize' for 'ise', the dropping of the full point after 'Mr' and 'Mrs', and the use of single rather than double quotes, in order to be consistent and to follow current standard usage.

SELECT BIBLIOGRAPHY

BIBLIOGRAPHY

KIRKPATRICK, B. J., *A Bibliography of Virginia Woolf* (2nd edn.; Oxford: University Press, 1980).

BIOGRAPHY

BELL, QUENTIN, *Virginia Woolf: A Biography* (2 vols.; London: Hogarth Press, 1972).

POOLE, ROGER, *The Unknown Virginia Woolf* (Cambridge: University Press, 1978).

ROSE, PHYLLIS, *Woman of Letters: A Life of Virginia Woolf* (New York: Oxford University Press, 1978).

WOOLF, LEONARD, *An Autobiography* (2 vols.; Oxford: University Press, 1980).

EDITIONS

The Diary of Virginia Woolf, ed. Anne Olivier Bell, assisted by Andrew McNeillie (5 vols.; London: Hogarth Press, 1977–84).

The Letters of Virginia Woolf, ed. Nigel Nicolson and Joanne Trautmann (6 vols.; London: Hogarth Press, 1975–84).

GENERAL CRITICISM

BENNETT, JOAN, *Virginia Woolf: Her Art as a Novelist* (Cambridge: University Press, 1945, 1964).

BOWLBY, RACHEL, *Virginia Woolf: Feminist Destinations* (Oxford: Blackwell, 1988).

BREWSTER, DOROTHY, *Virginia Woolf* (London: Allen and Unwin, 1963).

DI BATTISTA, MARIA, *Virginia Woolf's Major Novels* (New Haven, Conn., and London: Yale University Press, 1980).

FLEISHMAN, AVROM, *Virginia Woolf: A Critical Reading* (Baltimore, Johns Hopkins University Press, 1977).

Select Bibliography

FREEDMAN, RALPH, *Virginia Woolf: Revaluation and Continuity* (Berkeley: University of California Press, 1980).

GUIGET, JEAN, *Virginia Woolf and her Works*, trans. Jean Stewart (London, Hogarth Press, 1965).

LEASKA, MITCHELL A., *The Novels of Virginia Woolf* (New York: John Jay Press, 1977).

LEE, HERMIONE, *The Novels of Virginia Woolf* (London: Methuen, 1977).

MAJUMDAR, ROBIN, and McLAURIN, ALLEN (eds.), *Virginia Woolf: The Critical Heritage* (London: Routledge and Kegan Paul, 1975).

MARCUS, JANE (ed.), *New Feminist Essays on Virginia Woolf* (London: Macmillan, 1981).

MARDER, HERBERT, *Feminism and Art: A Study of Virginia Woolf* (New Haven, Conn., and London: Yale University Press, 1968).

McLAURIN, ALLEN, *Virginia Woolf: The Echoes Enslaved* (Cambridge: University Press, 1973).

MINOW-PINKNEY, MAKIKO, *Virginia Woolf and the Problem of the Subject* (Brighton: Harvester, 1987).

MOODY, A. D., *Virginia Woolf* (Edinburgh: Oliver and Boyd, 1963).

THAKUR, N. C., *The Symbolism of Virginia Woolf* (London: Oxford University Press, 1965).

WARNER, ERIC (ed.), *Virginia Woolf: A Centenary Perspective* (London: Macmillan, 1984).

ZWERDLING, ALEX, *Virginia Woolf and the Real World* (Berkeley: University of California Press, 1986).

ON *BETWEEN THE ACTS*

BASHAM, C., '*Between the Acts*', *Durham University Journal*, 52 (1959), 87–94.

BEER, GILLIAN, 'Virginia Woolf and Pre-History', in Eric Warner (ed.), *Virginia Woolf: A Centenary Perspective* (London: Macmillan, 1984).

GILLESPIE, DIANE T., 'Virginia Woolf's Miss La Trobe: The

Select Bibliography

Artist's Last Struggle against Masculine Values', *Women and Literature*, 5 (1977), 38–46.

KENNEY, SUSAN M., 'Two Endings: Virginia Woolf's Suicide and *Between the Acts*', *University of Toronto Quarterly*, 4 (1975), 265–89.

MAIKA, PATRICIA, *Virginia Woolf's Between the Acts and Jane Harrison's Conspiracy* (Ann Arbor and London: UMI Research Press, 1987).

A CHRONOLOGY OF VIRGINIA WOOLF

Life	Historical and Cultural Background
1882 (25 Jan.) Adeline Virginia Stephen (VW) born at 22 Hyde Park Gate, London.	Deaths of Darwin, Trollope, D. G. Rossetti; Joyce born; Stravinsky born; Married Women's Property Act; Society for Psychical Research founded.
1895 (5 May) Death of mother, Julia Stephen; VW's first breakdown occurs soon afterwards.	Death of T. H. Huxley; X-rays discovered; invention of the cinematograph; wireless telegraphy invented; arrest, trials, and conviction of Oscar Wilde. Wilde, *The Importance of Being Earnest* and *An Ideal Husband* Wells, *The Time Machine*
1896 (Nov.) Travels in France with sister Vanessa.	Death of William Morris; *Daily Mail* started. Hardy, *Jude the Obscure* Housman, *A Shropshire Lad*
1897 (10 April) Marriage of half-sister Stella; (19 July) death of Stella; (Nov.) VW learning Greek and History at King's College, London.	Queen Victoria's Diamond Jubilee; Tate Gallery opens. Stoker, *Dracula* James, *What Maisie Knew*
1898	Deaths of Gladstone and Lewis Carroll; radium and plutonium discovered. Wells, *The War of the Worlds*
1899 (30 Oct.) VW's brother Thoby goes up to Trinity College, Cambridge, where he forms friendships with Lytton Strachey, Leonard Woolf, Clive Bell, and others of the future Bloomsbury Group (VW's younger brother Adrian follows him to Trinity in 1902).	Boer War begins. Births of Bowen and Coward. Symons, *The Symbolist Movement in Literature* James, *The Awkward Age* Freud, *The Interpretation of Dreams*
1900	Deaths of Nietzsche, Wilde, and Ruskin; *Daily Express* started; Planck announces quantum theory; Boxer Rising. Conrad, *Lord Jim*

Chronology

1901   Death of Queen Victoria; accession of Edward VII; first wireless communication between Europe and USA; 'World's Classics' series begun.
Kipling, *Kim*

1902 VW starts private lessons in Greek with Janet Case.   End of Boer War; British Academy founded; *Encyclopaedia Britannica* (10th edn.); *TLS* started.
Bennett, *Anna of the Five Towns*
James, *The Wings of the Dove*

1903   Deaths of Gissing and Spencer; *Daily Mirror* started; Wright brothers make their first aeroplane flight; Emmeline Pankhurst founds Women's Social and Political Union.
Butler, *The Way of All Flesh*
James, *The Ambassadors*
Moore, *Principia Ethica*

1904 (22 Feb.) Death of father, Sir Leslie Stephen. In spring, VW travels to Italy with Vanessa and friend Violet Dickinson. (10 May) VW has second nervous breakdown and is ill for three months. Moves to 46, Gordon Square. (14 Dec.) VW's first publication appears.   Deaths of Christina Rossetti and Chekhov; Russo-Japanese War; *Entente Cordiale* between Britain and France.
Chesterton, *The Napoleon of Notting Hill*
Conrad, *Nostromo*
James, *The Golden Bowl*

1905 (March, April) Travels in Portugal and Spain. Writes reviews and teaches once a week at Morley College, London.   Einstein, *Special Theory of Relativity*; Sartre born.
Shaw, *Major Barbara* and *Man and Superman*
Wells, *Kipps*
Forster, *Where Angels Fear to Tread*

1906 (Sept. and Oct.) Travels in Greece. (20 Nov.) death of Thoby Stephen.   Death of Ibsen; Beckett born; Liberal Government elected; Campbell-Bannerman Prime Minister; launch of HMS *Dreadnought*.

1907 (7 Feb.) Marriage of Vanessa to Clive Bell. VW moves with Adrian to 29 Fitzroy Square. At work on her first novel, 'Melymbrosia' (working title for *The Voyage Out*).   Auden born; Anglo-Russian Entente.
Synge, *The Playboy of the Western World*
Conrad, *The Secret Agent*
Forster, *The Longest Journey*

1908 (Sept.) Visits Italy with the Bells.	Asquith Prime Minister; Old Age Pensions Act; Elgar's First Symphony. Bennett, *The Old Wives' Tale* Forster, *A Room with a View* Chesterton, *The Man Who Was Thursday*
1909 (17 Feb.) Lytton Strachey proposes marriage. (30 March) First meets Lady Ottoline Morrell. (April) Visits Florence. (Aug.) Visits Bayreuth and Dresden.	Death of Meredith; 'People's Budget'; English Channel flown by Blériot. Wells, *Tono-Bungay* Masterman, *The Condition of England* Marinetti, *Futurist Manifesto*
1910 (Jan.) Works for women's suffrage. (June–Aug.) Spends time in a nursing home at Twickenham.	Deaths of Edward VII, Tolstoy, and Florence Nightingale; accession of George V; *Encyclopaedia Britannica* (11th edn.); Roger Fry's Post-Impressionist Exhibition. Bennett, *Clayhanger* Forster, *Howards End* Yeats, *The Green Helmet* Wells, *The History of Mr Polly*
1911 (April) Travels to Turkey, where Vanessa is ill. (Nov.) Moves to 38 Brunswick Square, sharing house with Adrian, John Maynard Keynes, Duncan Grant, and Leonard Woolf.	National Insurance Act; Suffragette riots. Conrad, *Under Western Eyes* Wells, *The New Machiavelli* Lawrence, *The White Peacock*
1912 Rents Asheham House. (Feb.) Spends some days in Twickenham nursing home. (10 Aug.) Marriage to Leonard Woolf. Honeymoon in Provence, Spain, and Italy. (Oct.) Moves to 13 Clifford's Inn, London.	Second Post-Impressionist Exhibition; Suffragettes active; strikes by dockers, coal-miners, and transport workers; Irish Home Rule Bill rejected by Lords; sinking of SS *Titanic*; death of Scott in the Antarctic; *Daily Herald* started. English translations of Chekhov and Dostoevsky begin to appear.
1913 (March) MS of *The Voyage Out* delivered to publisher. Unwell most of summer. (9 Sept.) Suicide attempt. Remains under care of nurses and husband for rest of year.	*New Statesman* started; Suffragettes active. Lawrence, *Sons and Lovers*

Chronology

1914   (16 Feb.) Last nurse leaves. Moves to Richmond, Surrey.

Irish Home Rule Bill passed by Parliament; First World War begins (4 Aug.); Dylan Thomas born.
Lewis, *Blast*
Joyce, *Dubliners*
Yeats, *Responsibilities*
Hardy, *Satires of Circumstance*
Bell, *Art*

1915   Purchase of Hogarth House, Richmond. (26 March) *The Voyage Out* published. (April, May) Bout of violent madness; under care of nurses until November.

Death of Rupert Brooke; Einstein, *General Theory of Relativity*; Second Battle of Ypres; Dardanelles Campaign; sinking of SS *Lusitania*; air attacks on London.
Ford, *The Good Soldier*
Lawrence, *The Rainbow*
Brooke, *1914 and Other Poems*
Richardson, *Pointed Roofs*

1916   (17 Oct.) Lectures to Richmond branch of the Women's Co-operative Guild. Regular work for *TLS*.

Death of James; Lloyd George Prime Minister; First Battle of the Somme; Battle of Verdun; Gallipoli Campaign; Easter Rising in Dublin.
Joyce, *Portrait of the Artist as a Young Man*

1917   (July) Hogarth Press commences publication with *The Mark on the Wall*. VW begins work on *Night and Day*.

Death of Edward Thomas. Third Battle of Ypres (Passchendaele); T. E. Lawrence's campaigns in Arabia; USA enters the War; Revolution in Russia (Feb., Oct.); Balfour Declaration.
Eliot, *Prufrock and Other Observations*

1918   Writes reviews and *Night and Day*; also sets type for the Hogarth Press. (15 Nov.) First meets T. S. Eliot.

Death of Owen; Second Battle of the Somme; final German offensive collapses; Armistice with Germany (11 Nov.); Franchise Act grants vote to women over 30; influenza pandemic kills millions.
Lewis, *Tarr*
Hopkins, *Poems*
Strachey, *Eminent Victorians*

1919   (1 July) Purchase of Monk's House, Rodmell, Sussex. (20 Oct.) *Night and Day* published.

Treaty of Versailles; Alcock and Brown fly the Atlantic; National Socialists founded in Germany.
Sinclair, *Mary Olivier*
Shaw, *Heartbreak House*

1920   Works on journalism and *Jacob's Room*.

League of Nations established.
Pound, *Hugh Selwyn Mauberley*
Lawrence, *Women in Love*
Eliot, *The Sacred Wood*
Fry, *Vision and Design*

[xlii]

Chronology

1921	Ill for summer months. (4 Nov.) Finishes *Jacob's Room*.	Irish Free State founded. Huxley, *Crome Yellow*
1922	(Jan. to May) Ill. (14 Dec.) First meets Vita Sackville-West. (24 Oct.) *Jacob's Room* published.	Bonar Law Prime Minister; Mussolini forms Fascist Government in Italy; death of Proust; *Encyclopaedia Britannica* (12th edn.); *Criterion* founded; BBC founded; Irish Free State proclaimed. Eliot, *The Waste Land* Galsworthy, *The Forsyte Saga* Joyce, *Ulysses* Mansfield, *The Garden Party* Wittgenstein, *Tractatus Logico-Philosophicus*
1923	(March, April) Visits Spain. Works on 'The Hours', the first version of *Mrs Dalloway*.	Baldwin Prime Minister; BBC radio begins broadcasting (Nov.); death of K. Mansfield.
1924	Purchase of lease on 52 Tavistock Square, Bloomsbury. Gives lecture that becomes 'Mr Bennett and Mrs Brown'. (8 Oct.) Finishes *Mrs Dalloway*.	First (minority) Labour Government; Ramsay MacDonald Prime Minister; deaths of Lenin, Kafka, and Conrad. Ford, *Some Do Not* Forster, *A Passage to India* O'Casey, *Juno and the Paycock* Coward, *The Vortex*
1925	(23 April) *The Common Reader* published. (14 May) *Mrs Dalloway* published. Ill during summer.	Gerhardie, *The Polyglots* Ford, *No More Parades* Huxley, *Those Barren Leaves* Whitehead, *Science and the Modern World*
1926	(Jan) Unwell with German measles. Writes *To the Lighthouse*.	General Strike (3–12 May); *Encyclopaedia Britannica* (13th edn.); first television demonstration. Ford, *A Man Could Stand Up* Tawney, *Religion and the Rise of Capitalism*
1927	(March, April) Travels in France and Italy. (5 May) *To the Lighthouse* published. (5 Oct.) Begins *Orlando*.	Lindburgh flies solo across the Atlantic; first 'talkie' films.
1928	(11 Oct.) *Orlando* published. Delivers lectures at Cambridge on which she bases *A Room of One's Own*.	Death of Hardy; votes for women over 21. Yeats, *The Tower* Lawrence, *Lady Chatterley's Lover* Waugh, *Decline and Fall* Sherriff, *Journey's End* Ford, *Last Post* Huxley, *Point Counter Point* Bell, *Civilization*

1929	(Jan.) Travels to Berlin. (24 Oct.) *A Room of One's Own* published.	2nd Labour Government, MacDonald Prime Minister; collapse of New York Stock Exchange; start of world economic depression. Graves, *Goodbye to All That* Aldington, *Death of a Hero* Green, *Living*
1930	(20 Feb.) First meets Ethel Smyth; (29 May) Finishes first version of *The Waves*.	Mass unemployment; television starts in USA; deaths of Lawrence and Conan Doyle. Auden, *Poems* Eliot, *Ash Wednesday* Waugh, *Vile Bodies* Coward, *Private Lives* Lewis, *Apes of God*
1931	(April) Car tour through France. (8 Oct.) *The Waves* published. Writes *Flush*.	Formation of National Government; abandonment of Gold Standard; death of Bennett; Japan invades China.
1932	(21 Jan.) Death of Lytton Strachey. (13 Oct.) *The Common Reader*, 2nd series, published. Begins *The Years*, at this point called 'The Pargiters'.	Roosevelt becomes President of USA; hunger marches start in Britain; *Scrutiny* starts. Huxley, *Brave New World*
1933	(May) Car tour of France and Italy. (5 Oct.) *Flush* published.	Deaths of Galsworthy and George Moore; Hitler becomes Chancellor of Germany. Orwell, *Down and Out in Paris and London* Wells, *The Shape of Things to Come.*
1934	Works on *The Years*. (9 Sept.) Death of Roger Fry.	Waugh, *A Handful of Dust* Graves, *I, Claudius* Beckett, *More Pricks than Kicks* Toynbee, *A Study of History*
1935	Rewrites *The Years*. (May) Car tour of Holland, Germany, and Italy.	George V's Silver Jubilee; Baldwin Prime Minister of National Government; Germany re-arms; Italian invasion of Abyssinia (Ethiopia). Isherwood, *Mr Norris Changes Trains* T. S. Eliot, *Murder in the Cathedral*
1936	(May–Oct.) Ill. Finishes *The Years*. Begins *Three Guineas*.	Death of George V; accession of Edward VIII; abdication crisis; accession of George VI; Civil War breaks out in Spain; first of the Moscow show trials; Germany re-occupies the Rhineland; BBC television begins (2 Nov); deaths of Chesterton, Kipling, and Housman. Orwell, *Keep the Aspidistra Flying*

1937 (15 March) *The Years* published. Begins *Roger Fry: A Biography*. (18 July) Death in Spanish Civil War of Julian Bell, son of Vanessa.

Chamberlain Prime Minister; destruction of Guernica; death of Barrie.
Orwell, *The Road to Wigan Pier*

1938 (2 June) *Three Guineas* published. Works on *Roger Fry*, and begins to envisage *Between the Acts*.

German *Anschluss* with Austria; Munich agreement; dismemberment of Czechoslovakia; first jet engine.
Beckett, *Murphy*
Bowen, *The Death of the Heart*
Greene, *Brighton Rock*

1939 VW moves to 37 Mecklenburgh Square, but lives mostly at Monk's House. Works on *Between the Acts*. Meets Freud in London.

End of Civil War in Spain; Russo-German pact; Germany invades Poland (Sept.); Britain and France declare war on Germany (3 Sept.); deaths of Freud, Yeats, and Ford.
Joyce, *Finnegans Wake*
Isherwood, *Goodbye to Berlin*

1940 (25 July) *Roger Fry* published. (10 Sept.) Mecklenburgh Square house bombed. (18 Oct.) witnesses the ruins of 52 Tavistock Square, destroyed by bombs. (23 Nov.) Finishes *Between the Acts*.

Germany invades north-west Europe; fall of France; evacuation of British troops from Dunkirk; Battle of Britain; beginning of 'the Blitz'; National Government under Churchill.

1941 (26 Feb.) Revises *Between the Acts*. Becomes ill. (28 March) Drowns herself in River Ouse, near Monk's House. (July) *Between the Acts* published.

Germany invades USSR; Japanese destroy US Fleet at Pearl Harbor; USA enters war; death of Joyce.

Between the Acts

IT was a summer's night and they were talking, in the big room with the windows open to the garden, about the cesspool. The county council had promised to bring water to the village, but they hadn't.

Mrs Haines, the wife of the gentleman farmer, a goosefaced woman with eyes protruding as if they saw something to gobble in the gutter, said affectedly: 'What a subject to talk about on a night like this!'

Then there was silence; and a cow coughed; and that led her to say how odd it was, as a child, she had never feared cows, only horses. But, then, as a small child in a perambulator, a great cart-horse had brushed within an inch of her face. Her family, she told the old man in the arm-chair, had lived near Liskeard* for many centuries. There were the graves in the churchyard to prove it.

A bird chuckled outside. 'A nightingale?' asked Mrs Haines. No, nightingales didn't come so far north. It was a daylight bird, chuckling over the substance and succulence of the day, over worms, snails, grit, even in sleep.

The old man in the arm-chair—Mr Oliver, of the Indian Civil Service, retired—said that the site they had chosen for the cesspool was, if he had heard aright, on the Roman road. From an aeroplane, he said, you could still see, plainly marked, the scars made by the Britons; by the Romans; by the

[3]

Elizabethan manor house; and by the plough, when
they ploughed the hill to grow wheat in the Napo-
leonic wars.

'But you don't remember . . .' Mrs Haines began.
No, not that. Still he did remember——and he was
about to tell them what, when there was a sound
outside, and Isa, his son's wife, came in with her hair
in pigtails; she was wearing a dressing-gown with
faded peacocks on it. She came in like a swan swimming its way; then was checked and stopped; was
surprised to find people there; and lights burning.
She had been sitting with her little boy who wasn't
well, she apologized. What had they been saying?

'Discussing the cesspool,' said Mr Oliver.

'What a subject to talk about on a night like this!'
Mrs Haines exclaimed again.

What had *he* said about the cesspool; or indeed
about anything? Isa wondered, inclining her head
towards the gentleman farmer, Rupert Haines. She
had met him at a Bazaar; and at a tennis party. He
had handed her a cup and a racquet—that was all.
But in his ravaged face she always felt mystery; and
in his silence, passion. At the tennis party she had felt
this, and at the Bazaar. Now a third time, if anything
more strongly, she felt it again.

'I remember,' the old man interrupted, 'my mother
. . .' Of his mother he remembered that she was very
stout; kept the tea-caddy locked;* yet had given him
in that very room a copy of Byron. It was over sixty

years ago, he told them, that his mother had given him the works of Byron in that very room. He paused.

'She walks in beauty like the night,' he quoted.

Then began:

'So we'll go no more a-roving by the light of the moon.'

Isa raised her head. The words made two rings, perfect rings, that floated them, herself and Haines, like two swans down stream. But his snow-white breast was circled with a tangle of dirty duckweed; and she too, in her webbed feet was entangled, by her husband the stockbroker. Sitting on her three-cornered chair she swayed, with her dark pigtails hanging, and her body like a bolster in its faded dressing-gown.

Mrs Haines was aware of the emotion circling them, excluding her. She waited, as one waits for the strain of an organ to die out before leaving church. In the car going home to the red villa in the cornfields, she would destroy it, as a thrush pecks the wings off a butterfly. Allowing ten seconds to intervene, she rose; paused; and then, as if she had heard the last strain die out, offered Mrs Giles Oliver her hand.

But Isa, though she should have risen at the same moment that Mrs Haines rose, sat on. Mrs Haines glared at her out of goose-like eyes, gobbling, 'Please, Mrs Giles Oliver, do me the kindness to recognize my existence . . .' which she was forced to do, rising at last from her chair, in her faded dressing-gown, with the pigtails falling over each shoulder.

Pointz Hall was seen in the light of an early summer morning to be a middle-sized house. It did not rank among the houses that are mentioned in guide books. It was too homely. But this whitish house with the grey roof, and the wing thrown out at right angles, lying unfortunately low on the meadow with a fringe of trees on the bank above it so that smoke curled up to the nests of the rooks, was a desirable house to live in. Driving past, people said to each other: 'I wonder if that'll ever come into the market?' And to the chauffeur: 'Who lives there?'

The chauffeur didn't know. The Olivers, who had bought the place something over a century ago, had no connection with the Warings, the Elveys, the Mannerings or the Burnets; the old families who had all intermarried, and lay in their deaths inter-twisted, like the ivy roots, beneath the churchyard wall.

Only something over a hundred and twenty years the Olivers had been there. Still, on going up the principal staircase—there was another, a mere ladder at the back for the servants—there was a portrait. A length of yellow brocade was visible half-way up; and, as one reached the top, a small powdered face, a great head-dress slung with pearls, came into view;

[6]

an ancestress of sorts. Six or seven bedrooms opened
out of the corridor. The butler had been a soldier;
had married a lady's maid; and, under a glass case
there was a watch that had stopped a bullet on the
field of Waterloo.

It was early morning. The dew was on the grass.
The church clock struck eight times. Mrs Swithin
drew the curtain in her bedroom—the faded white
chintz that so agreeably from the outside tinged the
window with its green lining. There with her old
hands on the hasp, jerking it open, she stood: old
Oliver's married sister; a widow. She always meant
to set up a house of her own; perhaps in Kensington,
perhaps at Kew, so that she could have the benefit of
the gardens.* But she stayed on all through the
summer; and when winter wept its damp upon the
panes, and choked the gutters with dead leaves, she
said: 'Why, Bart, did they build the house in the
hollow, facing north?' Her brother said, 'Obviously
to escape from nature. Weren't four horses needed to
drag the family coach through the mud?' Then he
told her the famous story of the great eighteenth-
century winter; when for a whole month the house
had been blocked by snow. And the trees had fallen.
So every year, when winter came, Mrs Swithin retired
to Hastings.*

But it was summer now. She had been waked by
the birds. How they sang! attacking the dawn like so
many choir boys attacking an iced cake. Forced to

listen, she had stretched for her favourite reading— an Outline of History*—and had spent the hours between three and five thinking of rhododendron forests in Piccadilly; when the entire continent, not then, she understood, divided by a channel, was all one; populated, she understood, by elephant-bodied, seal-necked, heaving, surging, slowly writhing, and, she supposed, barking monsters; the iguanodon, the mammoth, and the mastodon; from whom presumably, she thought, jerking the window open, we descend.

It took her five seconds in actual time, in mind time ever so much longer, to separate Grace herself, with blue china on a tray, from the leather-covered grunting monster who was about, as the door opened, to demolish a whole tree in the green steaming undergrowth of the primeval forest. Naturally she jumped, as Grace put the tray down and said: 'Good morning, Ma'am.' 'Batty,' Grace called her, as she felt on her face the divided glance that was half meant for a beast in a swamp, half for a maid in a print frock and white apron.

'How those birds sing!' said Mrs Swithin, at a venture. The window was open now; the birds certainly were singing. An obliging thrush hopped across the lawn; a coil of pinkish rubber twisted in its beak. Tempted by the sight to continue her imaginative reconstruction of the past, Mrs Swithin paused; she was given to increasing the bounds of the moment by flights into past or future; or sidelong down corridors and alleys; but she remembered her mother—her mother in that very room rebuking her. 'Don't stand gaping, Lucy, or the wind'll change . . .' How often her mother had rebuked her in that very room—'but in a very different world', as her brother would remind her. So she sat down to morning tea, like any other old lady with a high nose, thin cheeks, a ring on her finger and the usual trappings of rather shabby but gallant old age, which included in her case a cross gleaming gold on her breast.

The nurses after breakfast were trundling the perambulator up and down the terrace; and as they trundled they were talking—not shaping pellets of information or handing ideas from one to another, but rolling words, like sweets on their tongues; which, as they thinned to transparency, gave off pink, green, and sweetness. This morning that sweetness was: 'How cook had told 'im off about the asparagus; how when she rang I said: how it was a sweet costume with blouse to match;' and that was leading to something about a feller as they walked up and down the terrace rolling sweets, trundling the perambulator.

It was a pity that the man who had built Pointz Hall had pitched the house in a hollow, when beyond the flower garden and the vegetables there was this stretch of high ground. Nature had provided a site for a house; man had built his house in a hollow. Nature had provided a stretch of turf half a mile in length and level, till it suddenly dipped to the lily pool. The terrace was broad enough to take the entire shadow of one of the great trees laid flat. There you could walk up and down, up and down, under the shade of the trees. Two or three grew close together, then there were gaps. Their roots broke the turf, and among those bones were green waterfalls and cushions of grass in which violets grew in spring or in summer the wild purple orchis.

Amy was saying something about a feller when Mabel, with her hand on the pram, turned sharply, her sweet swallowed. 'Leave off grubbing,' she said sharply. 'Come along, George.'

The little boy had lagged and was grouting in the grass. Then the baby, Caro, thrust her fist out over the coverlet and the furry bear was jerked overboard. Amy had to stoop. George grubbed. The flower blazed between the angles of the roots. Membrane after membrane was torn. It blazed a soft yellow, a lambent light under a film of velvet; it filled the caverns behind the eyes with light. All that inner darkness became a hall, leaf smelling, earth smelling of yellow light. And the tree was beyond the flower; the grass, the flower and the tree were entire. Down on his knees grubbing he held the flower complete. Then there was a roar and a hot breath and a stream of coarse grey hair rushed between him and the flower. Up he leapt, toppling in his fright, and saw coming towards him a terrible peaked eyeless monster moving on legs, brandishing arms.

'Good morning, sir,' a hollow voice boomed at him from a beak of paper.

The old man had sprung upon him from his hiding-place behind a tree.

'Say good morning, George; say "Good morning, Grandpa,"' Mabel urged him, giving him a push towards the man. But George stood gaping. George stood gazing. Then Mr Oliver crumpled the paper which he had cocked into a snout and appeared in person. A very tall old man, with gleaming eyes, wrinkled cheeks, and a head with no hair on it. He turned.

'Heel!' he bawled, 'heel, you brute!' And George turned; and the nurses turned holding the furry bear; they all turned to look at Sohrab the Afghan hound bounding and bouncing among the flowers.

'Heel!' the old man bawled, as if he were commanding a regiment. It was impressive, to the nurses, the way an old boy of his age could still bawl and make a brute like that obey him. Back came the Afghan hound, sidling, apologetic. And as he cringed at the old man's feet, a string was slipped over his collar; the noose that old Oliver always carried with him.

'You wild beast ... you bad beast,' he grumbled, stooping. George looked at the dog only. The hairy flanks were sucked in and out; there was a blob of foam on its nostrils. He burst out crying.

Old Oliver raised himself, his veins swollen, his cheeks flushed; he was angry. His little game with the paper hadn't worked. The boy was a cry-baby. He nodded and sauntered on, smoothing out the crumpled paper and muttering, as he tried to find his line in the column, 'A cry-baby—a cry-baby.' But the breeze blew the great sheet out; and over the edge he surveyed the landscape—flowing fields, heath and woods. Framed, they became a picture. Had he been a painter, he would have fixed his easel here, where the country, barred by trees, looked like a picture. Then the breeze fell.

'M. Daladier',* he read finding his place in the column, 'has been successful in pegging down the franc . . .'

Mrs Giles Oliver drew the comb through the thick tangle of hair which, after giving the matter her best attention, she had never had shingled or bobbed; and lifted the heavily embossed silver brush that had been a wedding present and had its uses in impressing chambermaids in hotels. She lifted it and stood in front of the three-folded mirror, so that she could see three separate versions of her rather heavy, yet handsome, face; and also, outside the glass, a slip of terrace, lawn and tree tops.

Inside the glass, in her eyes, she saw what she had felt overnight for the ravaged, the silent, the romantic gentleman farmer. 'In love,' was in her eyes. But outside, on the washstand, on the dressing-table, among the silver boxes and tooth-brushes, was the other love; love for her husband, the stockbroker— 'The father of my children', she added, slipping into the cliché conveniently provided by fiction. Inner love was in the eyes; outer love on the dressing-table. But what feeling was it that stirred in her now when above the looking-glass, out of doors, she saw coming across the lawn the perambulator; two nurses; and her little boy George, lagging behind?

She tapped on the window with her embossed hairbrush. They were too far off to hear. The drone of the trees was in their ears; the chirp of birds; other incidents of garden life, inaudible, invisible to her in the bedroom, absorbed them. Isolated on a green island, hedged about with snowdrops, laid with a counterpane of puckered silk, the innocent island floated under her window. Only George lagged behind.

She returned to her eyes in the looking-glass. 'In love', she must be; since the presence of his body in the room last night could so affect her; since the words he said, handing her a teacup, handing her a tennis racquet, could so attach themselves to a certain spot in her; and thus lie between them like a wire, tingling, tangling, vibrating—she groped, in the

depths of the looking-glass, for a word to fit the
infinitely quick vibrations of the aeroplane propeller
that she had seen once at dawn at Croydon.* Faster,
faster, faster, it whizzed, whirred, buzzed, till all the
flails became one flail and up soared the plane away
and away . . .

'Where we know not, where we go not, neither
know nor care,' she hummed. 'Flying, rushing
through the ambient, incandescent, summer
silent . . .'

The rhyme was 'air'. She put down her brush. She
took up the telephone.

'Three, four, eight, Pyecombe,' she said.

'Mrs Oliver speaking . . . What fish have you this
morning? Cod? Halibut? Sole? Plaice?'

'There to lose what binds us here,' she murmured.
'Soles. Filleted. In time for lunch please,' she said
aloud. 'With a feather, a blue feather . . . flying
mounting through the air . . . there to lose what binds
us here . . .' The words weren't worth writing in the
book bound like an account book in case Giles
suspected. 'Abortive', was the word that expressed
her. She never came out of a shop, for example, with
the clothes she admired; nor did her figure, seen
against the dark roll of trousering in a shop window,
please her. Thick of waist, large of limb, and save for
her hair, fashionable in the tight modern way, she
never looked like Sappho, or one of the beautiful
young men whose photographs adorned the weekly

papers. She looked what she was: Sir Richard's daughter; and niece of the two old ladies at Wimbledon who were so proud, being O'Neils,* of their descent from the Kings of Ireland.

A foolish, flattering lady, pausing on the threshold of what she once called 'the heart of the house', the threshold of the library, had once said: 'Next to the kitchen, the library's always the nicest room in the house.' Then she added, stepping across the threshold: 'Books are the mirrors of the soul.'

In this case a tarnished, a spotted soul. For as the train took over three hours to reach this remote village in the very heart of England, no one ventured so long a journey, without staving off possible mind-hunger, without buying a book on a bookstall. Thus the mirror that reflected the soul sublime, reflected also the soul bored. Nobody could pretend, as they looked at the shuffle of shilling shockers that week-enders had dropped, that the looking-glass always reflected the anguish of a Queen or the heroism of King Harry.

At this early hour of a June morning the library was empty. Mrs Giles had to visit the kitchen. Mr Oliver still tramped the terrace. And Mrs Swithin was of course at church. The light but variable breeze, foretold by the weather expert, flapped the yellow curtain, tossing light, then shadow. The fire greyed, then glowed, and the tortoiseshell butterfly beat on the lower pane of the window; beat, beat beat; repeating that if no human being ever came, never, never, never, the books would be mouldy, the fire out and the tortoiseshell butterfly dead on the pane.

Heralded by the impetuosity of the Afghan hound, the old man entered. He had read his paper; he was drowsy; and so sank down into the chintz-covered chair with the dog at his feet—the Afghan hound. His nose on his paws, his haunches drawn up, he looked a stone dog, a crusader's dog, guarding even in the realms of death the sleep of his master. But the master was not dead; only dreaming; drowsily, seeing as in a glass, its lustre spotted, himself, a young man helmeted; and a cascade falling. But no water; and the hills, like grey stuff pleated; and in the sand a hoop of ribs; a bullock maggot-eaten in the sun; and in the shadow of the rock, savages; and in his hand a gun. The dream hand clenched; the real hand lay on the chair arm, the veins swollen but only with a brownish fluid now.

The door opened.

'Am I', Isa apologized, 'interrupting?'

Of course she was—destroying youth and India. It was his fault, since she had persisted in stretching his thread of life so fine, so far. Indeed he was grateful to her, watching her as she strolled about the room, for continuing.

Many old men had only their India—old men in

[16]

clubs, old men in rooms off Jermyn Street. She in her striped dress continued him, murmuring, in front of the book cases: 'The moor is dark beneath the moon, rapid clouds have drunk the last pale beams of even . . . I have ordered the fish,' she said aloud, turning, 'though whether it'll be fresh or not I can't promise. But veal is dear, and everybody in the house is sick of beef and mutton . . . Sohrab,' she said, coming to a standstill in front of them, 'What's *he* been doing?'

His tail never wagged. He never admitted the ties of domesticity. Either he cringed or he bit. Now his wild yellow eyes gazed at her, gazed at him. He could outstare them both. Then Oliver remembered:

'Your little boy's a cry-baby,' he said scornfully.

'Oh,' she sighed, pegged down on a chair arm, like a captive balloon, by a myriad of hair-thin ties into domesticity. 'What's been happening?'

'I took the newspaper,' he exclaimed, 'so . . .'

He took it and crumpled it into a beak over his nose. 'So', he had sprung out from behind a tree on to the children.

'And he howled. He's a coward, your boy is.'

She frowned. He was not a coward, her boy wasn't. And she loathed the domestic, the possessive; the maternal. And he knew it and did it on purpose to tease her, the old brute, her father-in-law.

She looked away.

'The library's always the nicest room in the house,' she quoted, and ran her eyes along the books. 'The

mirror of the soul' books were. *The Faerie Queene**
and Kinglake's *Crimea*;* Keats and the *Kreutzer
Sonata*.* There they were, reflecting. What? What
remedy was there for her at her age—the age of the
century, thirty-nine—in books? Book-shy she was,
like the rest of her generation; and gun-shy too. Yet
as a person with a raging tooth runs her eye in a
chemist shop over green bottles with gilt scrolls on
them lest one of them may contain a cure, she
considered: Keats and Shelley; Yeats and Donne. Or
perhaps not a poem; a life. The life of Garibaldi.* The
life of Lord Palmerston.* Or perhaps not a person's
life; a county's. *The Antiquities of Durham*; *The
Proceedings of the Archaeological Society of Nottingham*. Or not a life at all, but science—Eddington,* Darwin, or Jeans.*

None of them stopped her toothache. For her
generation the newspaper was a book; and, as her
father-in-law had dropped *The Times*, she took it and
read: 'A horse with a green tail . . .' which was
fantastic. Next, 'The guard at Whitehall* . . .' which
was romantic and then, building word upon word she
read: 'The troopers told her the horse had a green
tail; but she found it was just an ordinary horse. And
they dragged her up to the barrack room where she
was thrown upon a bed. Then one of the troopers
removed part of her clothing, and she screamed and
hit him about the face . . .'

That was real; so real that on the mahogany door

panels she saw the Arch in Whitehall; through the
Arch the barrack room; in the barrack room the bed,
and on the bed the girl was screaming and hitting him
about the face, when the door (for in fact it was a
door) opened and in came Mrs Swithin carrying a
hammer.

She advanced, sidling, as if the floor were fluid
under her shabby garden shoes, and, advancing,
pursed her lips and smiled, sidelong, at her brother.
Not a word passed between them as she went to the
cupboard in the corner and replaced the hammer,
which she had taken without asking leave, togeth.er—
she unclosed her fist—with a handful of nails.

'Cindy—Cindy,' he growled, as she shut the cupboard door.

Lucy, his sister, was three years younger than he
was. The name Cindy, or Sindy, for it could be spelt
either way, was short for Lucy. It was by this name
that he had called her when they were children; when
she had trotted after him as he fished, and had made
the meadow flowers into tight little bunches, winding
one long grass stalk round and round and round.
Once, she remembered, he had made her take the fish
off the hook herself. The blood had shocked her—
'Oh!' she had cried—for the gills were full of blood.
And he had growled: 'Cindy!' The ghost of that
morning in the meadow was in her mind as she
replaced the hammer where it belonged on one shelf;
and the nails where they belonged on another; and

[19]

shut the cupboard about which, for he still kept his
fishing tackle there, he was still so very particular.

'I've been nailing the placard on the Barn,' she said,
giving him a little pat on the shoulder.

The words were like the first peal of a chime of
bells. As the first peals, you hear the second; as the
second peals, you hear the third. So when Isa heard
Mrs Swithin say: 'I've been nailing the placard to the
Barn,' she knew she would say next:

'For the pageant.'

And he would say:

'Today? By Jupiter! I'd forgotten!'

'If it's fine,' Mrs Swithin continued, 'they'll act on
the terrace . . .'

'And if it's wet,' Bartholomew continued, 'in the
Barn.'

'And which will it be?' Mrs Swithin continued.
'Wet or fine?'

Then, for the seventh time in succession, they both
looked out of the window.

Every summer, for seven summers now, Isa had
heard the same words; about the hammer and the
nails; the pageant and the weather. Every year they
said, would it be wet or fine; and every year it was—
one or the other. The same chime followed the same
chime, only this year beneath the chime she heard:
'The girl screamed and hit him about the face with a
hammer.'

'The forecast', said Mr Oliver, turning the pages till

he found it, 'says: Variable winds; fair average temperature; rain at times.'

He put down the paper, and they all looked to the sky to see whether the sky obeyed the meteorologist. Certainly the weather was variable. It was green in the garden one moment; grey the next. Here came the sun—an illimitable rapture of joy, embracing every flower, every leaf. Then in compassion it withdrew, covering its face, as if it forebore to look on human suffering. There was a fecklessness, a lack of symmetry and order in the clouds, as they thinned and thickened. Was it their own law, or no law, they obeyed? Some were wisps of white hair merely. One, high up, very distant, had hardened to golden alabaster; was made of immortal marble. Beyond that was blue, pure blue, black blue; blue that had never filtered down; that had escaped registration. It never fell as sun, shadow, or rain upon the world, but disregarded the little coloured ball of earth entirely. No flower felt it; no field; no garden.

Mrs Swithin's eyes glazed as she looked at it. Isa thought her gaze was fixed because she saw God there, God on his throne. But as a shadow fell next moment on the garden Mrs Swithin loosed and lowered her fixed look and said:

'It's very unsettled. It'll rain, I'm afraid. We can only pray,' she added, and fingered her crucifix.

'And provide umbrellas,' said her brother.

Lucy flushed. He had struck her faith. When she

said 'pray', he added 'umbrellas'. She half covered the cross with her fingers. She shrank; she cowered; but next moment she exclaimed:

'Oh there they are—the darlings!'

The perambulator was passing across the lawn.

Isa looked too. What an angel she was—the old woman! Thus to salute the children; to beat up against those immensities and the old man's irreverences her skinny hands, her laughing eyes! How courageous to defy Bart and the weather!

'He looks blooming,' said Mrs Swithin.

'It's astonishing how they pick up,' said Isa.

'He ate his breakfast?' Mrs Swithin asked.

'Every scrap,' said Isa.

'And baby? No sign of measles?'

Isa shook her head. 'Touch wood,' she added, tapping the table.

'Tell me, Bart,' said Mrs Swithin turning to her brother, 'what's the origin of that? Touch wood . . . Antaeus, didn't he touch earth?'

She would have been, he thought, a very clever woman, had she fixed her gaze. But this led to that; that to the other. What went in at this ear, went out at that. And all were circled, as happens after seventy, by one recurring question. Hers was, should she live at Kensington or at Kew? But every year, when winter came, she did neither. She took lodgings at Hastings.

'Touch wood; touch earth; Antaeus,'* he muttered,

bringing the scattered bits together. Lemprière*
would settle it; or the Encyclopaedia. But it was not
in books the answer to his question—why, in Lucy's
skull, shaped so much like his own, there existed a
prayable being? She didn't, he supposed, invest it
with hair, teeth or toenails. It was, he supposed more
of a force or a radiance, controlling the thrush and
the worm; the tulip and the hound; and himself, too,
an old man with swollen veins. It got her out of bed
on a cold morning and sent her down the muddy path
to worship it, whose mouthpiece was Streatfield. A
good fellow, who smoked cigars in the vestry. He
needed some solace, doling out preachments to asth-
matic elders, perpetually repairing the perpetually
falling steeple, by means of placards nailed to Barns.
The love, he was thinking, that they should give to
flesh and blood they give to the church . . . when
Lucy rapping her fingers on the table said:

'What's the origin—the origin—of that?'

'Superstition,' he said.

She flushed, and the little breath too was audible
that she drew in as once more he struck a blow at her
faith. But, brother and sister, flesh and blood was not
a barrier, but a mist. Nothing changed their affection;
no argument; no fact; no truth. What she saw he didn't;
what he saw she didn't—and so on, *ad infinitum*.

'Cindy,' he growled. And the quarrel was over.

*

The Barn to which Lucy had nailed her placard was a great building in the farmyard. It was as old as the church, and built of the same stone, but it had no steeple. It was raised on cones of grey stone at the corners to protect it from rats and damp. Those who had been to Greece always said it reminded them of a temple. Those who had never been to Greece—the majority—admired it all the same. The roof was weathered red-orange; and inside it was a hollow hall, sunshafted, brown, smelling of corn, dark when the doors were shut, but splendidly illuminated when the doors at the end stood open, as they did to let the wagons in—the long low wagons, like ships of the sea, breasting the corn, not the sea, returning in the evening shagged with hay. The lanes caught tufts where the wagons had passed.

Now benches were drawn across the floor of the Barn. If it rained, the actors were to act in the Barn; planks had been laid together at one end to form a stage. Wet or fine, the audience would take tea there. Young men and women—Jim, Iris, David, Jessica— were even now busy with garlands of red and white paper roses left over from the Coronation.* The seeds and the dust from the sacks made them sneeze. Iris had a handkerchief bound round her forehead; Jessica wore breeches. The young men worked in shirt sleeves. Pale husks had stuck in their hair, and it was easy to run a splinter of wood into the fingers.

'Old Flimsy' (Mrs Swithin's nickname) had been

nailing another placard on the Barn. The first had been blown down, or the village idiot, who always tore down what had been nailed up, had done it, and was chuckling over the placard under the shade of some hedge. The workers were laughing too, as if old Swithin had left a wake of laughter behind her. The old girl with a wisp of white hair flying, knobbed shoes as if she had claws corned like a canary's, and black stockings wrinkled over the ankles, naturally made David cock his eye and Jessica wink back, as she handed him a length of paper roses. Snobs they were; long enough stationed that is in that one corner of the world to have taken indelibly the print of some three hundred years of customary behaviour. So they laughed; but respected. If she wore pearls, pearls they were.

'Old Flimsy on the hop,' said David. She would be in and out twenty times, and finally bring them lemonade in a great jug and a plate of sandwiches. Jessie held the garland; he hammered. A hen strayed in; a file of cows passed the door; then a sheep dog; then the cowman, Bond, who stopped.

He contemplated the young people hanging roses from one rafter to another. He thought very little of anybody, simples or gentry. Leaning, silent, sardonic, against the door he was like a withered willow, bent over a stream, all its leaves shed, and in his eyes the whimsical flow of the waters.

'Hi—huh!' he cried suddenly. It was cow language

presumably, for the parti-coloured cow, who had thrust her head in at the door lowered her horns, lashed her tail and ambled off. Bond followed after.

'That's the problem,' said Mrs Swithin. While Mr Oliver consulted the Encyclopaedia searching under Superstition for the origin of the expression 'Touch Wood', she and Isa discussed fish: whether, coming from a distance, it would be fresh.

They were so far from the sea. A hundred miles away, Mrs Swithin said; no, perhaps a hundred and fifty. 'But they do say', she continued, 'one can hear the waves on a still night. After a storm, they say, you can hear a wave break ... I like that story,' she reflected. 'Hearing the waves in the middle of the night he saddled a horse and rode to the sea. Who was it, Bart, who rode to the sea?'

He was reading.

'You can't expect it brought to your door in a pail of water,' said Mrs Swithin, 'as I remember when we were children, living in a house by the sea. Lobsters, fresh from the lobster pots. How they pinched the stick cook gave them! And salmon. You know if they're fresh because they have lice in their scales.'

Bartholomew nodded. A fact that was. He remembered, the house by the sea. And the lobster.

They were bringing up nets full of fish from the

sea; but Isa was seeing—the garden, variable as the forecast said, in the light breeze. Again, the children passed and she tapped on the window and blew them a kiss. In the drone of the garden it went unheeded.

'Are we really', she said, turning round, 'a hundred miles from the sea?'

'Thirty-five only,' her father-in-law said, as if he had whipped a tape measure from his pocket and measured it exactly.

'It seems more,' said Isa. 'It seems from the terrace as if the land went on for ever and ever.'

'Once there was no sea,' said Mrs Swithin. 'No sea at all between us and the continent. I was reading that in a book this morning. There were rhododendrons in the Strand; and mammoths in Piccadilly.'

'When we were savages,' said Isa.

Then she remembered; her dentist had told her that savages could perform very skilful operations on the brain. Savages had false teeth, he said. False teeth were invented, she thought he said, in the time of the Pharaohs.

'At least so my dentist told me,' she concluded.

'Which man d'you go to now?' Mrs Swithin asked her.

'The same old couple; Batty and Bates in Sloane Street.'

'And Mr Batty told you they had false teeth in the time of the Pharaohs?' Mrs Swithin pondered.

'Batty? Oh not Batty. Bates,' Isa corrected her.

Batty, she recalled, only talked about Royalty. Batty, she told Mrs Swithin, had a patient a Princess.

'So he kept me waiting well over an hour. And you know, when one's a child, how long that seems.'

'Marriages with cousins', said Mrs Swithin, 'can't be good for the teeth.'

Bart put his finger inside his mouth and projected the upper row outside his lips. They were false. Yet, he said, the Olivers hadn't married cousins. The Olivers couldn't trace their descent for more than two or three hundred years. But the Swithins could. The Swithins were there before the Conquest.

'The Swithins,' Mrs Swithin began. Then she stopped. Bart would crack another joke about Saints,* if she gave him the chance. And she had had two jokes cracked at her already; one about an umbrella; another about superstition.

So she stopped and said, 'How did we begin this talk?' She counted on her fingers. 'The Pharaohs. Dentists. Fish ... Oh yes, you were saying, Isa, you'd ordered fish; and you were afraid it wouldn't be fresh. And I said "That's the problem ..."'

The fish had been delivered. Mitchell's boy, holding them in a crook of his arm, jumped off his motor bike. There was no feeding the pony with lumps of sugar at the kitchen door, nor time for gossip, since his round had been increased. He had to deliver right over the hill at Bickley; also go round by Waythorn, Roddam, and Pyeminster,* whose names, like his own, were in Domesday Book.* But the cook—Mrs Sands she was called, but by old friends Trixie—had never in all her fifty years been over the hill, nor wanted to.

He dabbed them down on the kitchen table, the filleted soles, the semi-transparent boneless fish. And before Mrs Sands had time to peel the paper off, he was gone, giving a slap to the very fine yellow cat who rose majestically from the basket chair and advanced superbly to the table, winding the fish.

Were they a bit whiffy? Mrs Sands held them to her nose. The cat rubbed itself this way, that way against the table legs, against her legs. She would save a slice for Sunny—his drawing-room name Sung-Yen had undergone a kitchen change into Sunny. She took them, the cat attendant, to the larder, and laid them on a plate in that semi-ecclesiastical apartment. For the house before the Reformation, like so many houses in that neighbourhood, had a chapel; and the chapel had become a larder, changing, like the cat's name, as religion changed. The Master (his drawing-room name; in the kitchen they called him Bartie) would bring gentlemen sometimes to see the larder—often when cook wasn't dressed. Not to see the hams that hung from hooks, or the butter on a blue slate, or the joint for tomorrow's dinner, but to see the cellar that opened out of the larder and its carved

arch. If you tapped—one gentleman had a hammer—
there was a hollow sound; a reverberation; undoubt-
edly, he said, a concealed passage where once somebody had hid. So it might be. But Mrs Sands wished
they wouldn't come into her kitchen telling stories
with the girls about. It put ideas into their silly heads.
They heard dead men rolling barrels. They saw a
white lady walking under the tree. No one would
cross the terrace after dark. If a cat sneezed, 'There's
the ghost!'

Sunny had his little bit off the fillet. Then Mrs
Sands took an egg from the brown basket full of eggs;
some with yellow fluff sticking to the shells; then a
pinch of flour to coat those semi-transparent slips;
and a crust from the great earthenware crock full of
crusts. Then, returning to the kitchen, she made those
quick movements at the oven, cinder raking, stoking,
damping, which sent strange echoes through the
house, so that in the library, the sitting-room, the
dining-room, and the nursery, whatever they were
doing, thinking, saying, they knew, they all knew, it
was getting on for breakfast, lunch, or dinner.

'The sandwiches . . .' said Mrs Swithin, coming
into the kitchen. She refrained from adding 'Sands' to
'sandwiches', for Sands and sandwiches clashed.
'Never play', her mother used to say, 'on people's
names.' And Trixie was not a name that suited, as
Sands did, the thin, acid woman, red-haired, sharp
and clean, who never dashed off masterpieces, it was

true; but then never dropped hairpins in the soup. 'What in the name of Thunder?' Bart had said, raising a hairpin in his spoon, in the old days, fifteen years ago, before Sands came, in the time of Jessie Pook.

Mrs Sands fetched bread; Mrs Swithin fetched ham. One cut the bread; the other the ham. It was soothing, it was consolidating, this handwork together. The cook's hands cut, cut, cut. Whereas Lucy, holding the loaf, held the knife up. Why's stale bread, she mused, easier to cut than fresh? And so skipped, sidelong, from yeast to alcohol; so to fermentation; so to inebriation; so to Bacchus; and lay under purple lamps in a vineyard in Italy, as she had done, often; while Sands heard the clock tick; saw the cat; noted a fly buzz; and registered, as her lips showed, a grudge she mustn't speak against people making work in the kitchen while they had a high old time hanging paper roses in the barn.

'Will it be fine?' asked Mrs Swithin, her knife suspended. In the kitchen they humoured old Mother Swithin's fancies.

'Seems like it,' said Mrs Sands, giving her sharp look-out of the kitchen window.

'It wasn't last year,' said Mrs Swithin. 'D'you remember what a rush we had—when the rain came—getting in the chairs?' She cut again. Then she asked about Billy, Mrs Sands's nephew, apprenticed to the butcher.

'He's been doing', Mrs Sands said, 'what boys shouldn't; cheeking the master.'

'That'll be all right,' said Mrs Swithin, half meaning the boy, half meaning the sandwich, as it happened a very neat one, trimmed, triangular.

'Mr Giles may be late,' she added, laying it, complacently, on top of the pile.

For Isa's husband, the stockbroker, was coming from London. And the local train, which met the express train, arrived by no means punctually, even if he caught the early train which was by no means certain. In which case it meant—but what it meant to Mrs Sands, when people missed their trains, and she, whatever she might want to do, must wait, by the oven, keeping meat hot, no one knew.

'There!' said Mrs Swithin, surveying the sandwiches, some neat, some not, 'I'll take 'em to the barn.' As for the lemonade, she assumed, without a flicker of doubt, that Jane the kitchenmaid would follow after.

Candish paused in the dining-room to move a yellow rose. Yellow, white, carnation red—he placed them. He loved flowers, and arranging them, and placing the green sword or heart shaped leaf that came, fitly, between them. Queerly, he loved them, considering his gambling and drinking. The yellow rose went there. Now all was ready—silver and white, forks and napkins, and in the middle the splashed bowl of variegated roses. So, with one last look, he left the dining-room.

Two pictures hung opposite the window. In real life they had never met, the long lady and the man holding his horse by the rein. The lady was a picture, bought by Oliver because he liked the picture; the man was an ancestor. He had a name. He held the rein in his hand. He had said to the painter:

'If you want my likeness, dang it sir, take it when the leaves are on the trees.' There were leaves on the trees. He had said: 'Ain't there room for Colin as well as Buster?' Colin was his famous hound. But there was only room for Buster. It was, he seemed to say, addressing the company not the painter, a damned shame to leave out Colin whom he wished buried at his feet, in the same grave, about 1750; but that skunk the Reverend Whatshisname wouldn't allow it.

He was a talk producer, that ancestor. But the lady was a picture. In her yellow robe, leaning, with a pillar to support her, a silver arrow in her hand, and a feather in her hair, she led the eye up, down, from the curve to the straight, through glades of greenery and shades of silver, dun and rose into silence. The room was empty.

Empty, empty, empty; silent, silent, silent. The room was a shell, singing of what was before time was; a vase stood in the heart of the house, alabaster, smooth, cold, holding the still, distilled essence of emptiness, silence.

Across the hall a door opened. One voice, another voice, a third voice came wimpling and warbling: gruff—Bart's voice; quavering—Lucy's voice; middle-toned—Isa's voice. Their voices impetuously, impatiently, protestingly came across the hall saying: 'The train's late;' saying: 'Keep it hot;' saying: 'We won't, no Candish, we won't wait.'

Coming out from the library the voices stopped in the hall. They encountered an obstacle evidently; a rock. Utterly impossible was it, even in the heart of the country, to be alone? That was the shock. After that, the rock was raced round, embraced. If it was painful, it was essential. There must be society. Coming out of the library it was painful, but pleasant, to run slap into Mrs Manresa and an unknown young man with tow-coloured hair and a twisted face. No escape was possible; meeting was inevitable. Uninvited, unexpected, droppers-in, lured off the high road by the very same instinct that caused the sheep and the cows to desire propinquity, they had come. But they had brought a lunch basket. Here it was.

'We couldn't resist when we saw the name on the signpost,' Mrs Manresa began in her rich fluty voice. 'And this is a friend—William Dodge. We were going to sit all alone in a field. And I said: "Why not ask our dear friends", seeing the signpost, "to shelter us?" A seat at the table—that's all we want. We have our grub. We have our glasses. We ask nothing but—' society apparently, to be with her kind.

And she waved her hand upon which there was a glove, and under the glove it seemed rings, at old Mr Oliver.

He bowed deep over her hand; a century ago, he would have kissed it. In all this sound of welcome, protestation, apology and again welcome, there was an element of silence, supplied by Isabella, observing the unknown young man. He was of course a gentleman; witness socks and trousers; brainy—tie spotted, waistcoat undone; urban, professional, that is putty coloured, unwholesome; very nervous, exhibiting a twitch at this sudden introduction, and fundamentally infernally conceited, for he deprecated Mrs Manresa's effusion, yet was her guest.

Isa felt antagonized, yet curious. But when Mrs Manresa added, to make all ship-shape: 'He's an artist,' and when William Dodge corrected her: 'I'm a clerk in an office'—she thought he said Education or Somerset House*—she had her finger on the knot which had tied itself so tightly, almost to the extent of squinting, certainly of twitching, in his face.

Then they went in to lunch, and Mrs Manresa bubbled up, enjoying her own capacity to surmount, without turning a hair, this minor social crisis—this laying of two more places. For had she not complete faith in flesh and blood? and aren't we all flesh and blood? and how silly to make bones of trifles when we're all flesh and blood under the skin—men and women too! But she preferred men—obviously.

'Or what are your rings for, and your nails, and that really adorable little straw hat?' said Isabella addressing Mrs Manresa silently and thereby making silence add its unmistakable contribution to talk. Her hat, her rings, her finger nails red as roses, smooth as shells, were there for all to see. But not her life history. That was only scraps and fragments to all of them, excluding perhaps William Dodge, whom she called 'Bill' publicly—a sign perhaps that he knew more than they did. Some of the things that he knew—that she strolled the garden at midnight in silk pyjamas, had the loud speaker playing jazz, and a cocktail bar, of course they knew also. But nothing private; no strict biographical facts.

She had been born, but it was only gossip said so, in Tasmania: her grandfather had been exported for some hanky-panky mid-Victorian scandal; malversation of trusts was it? But the story got no further the only time Isabella heard it than 'exported', for the husband of the communicative lady—Mrs Blencowe of the Grange—took exception, pedantically, to 'exported', said 'expatriated' was more like it, but not the right word, which he had on the tip of his tongue, but couldn't get at. And so the story dwindled away. Sometimes she referred to an uncle, a Bishop. But he was thought to have been a Colonial Bishop only. They forgot and forgave very easily in the Colonies. Also it was said her diamonds and rubies had been dug out of the earth with his own hands by a 'husband' who was not Ralph Manresa. Ralph, a Jew, got up to look the very spit and image of the landed gentry, supplied from directing City companies— that was certain—tons of money; and they had no child. But surely with George the Sixth on the throne it was old fashioned, dowdy, savoured of moth-eaten furs, bugles, cameos and black-edged notepaper, to go ferreting into people's pasts?

'All I need', said Mrs Manresa ogling Candish, as if he were a real man, not a stuffed man, 'is a corkscrew.' She had a bottle of champagne, but no corkscrew.*

'Look, Bill,' she continued, cocking her thumb— she was opening the bottle—'at the pictures. Didn't I tell you you'd have a treat?'

Vulgar she was in her gestures, in her whole person, over-sexed, over-dressed for a picnic. But what a desirable, at least valuable, quality it was—for everybody felt, directly she spoke, 'She's said it, she's done it, not I,' and could take advantage of the breach of decorum, of the fresh air that blew in, to follow like leaping dolphins in the wake of an ice-breaking vessel. Did she not restore to old Bartholomew his spice islands, his youth?

'I told him', she went on, ogling Bart now, 'that he wouldn't look at our things' (of which they had heaps

[37]

and mountains) 'after yours. And I promised him you'd show him the—the——' here the champagne fizzed up and she insisted upon filling Bart's glass first. 'What is it all you learned gentlemen rave about? An arch? Norman? Saxon? Who's the last from school? Mr Giles?'

She ogled Isabella now, conferring youth upon her; but always when she spoke to women, she veiled her eyes, for they, being conspirators, saw through it.

So with blow after blow, with champagne and ogling, she staked out her claim to be a wild child of nature, blowing into this—she did give one secret smile—sheltered harbour; which did make her smile, after London; yet it did, too, challenge London. For on she went to offer them a sample of her life; a few gobbets of gossip; mere trash; but she gave it for what it was worth; how last Tuesday she had been sitting next so and so; and she added, very casually a Christian name; then a nickname; and he'd said—for, as a mere nobody they didn't mind what they said to her—and 'in strict confidence, I needn't tell you,' she told them. And they all pricked their ears. And then, with a gesture of her hands as if tossing overboard that odious crackling-under-the-pot London life— so—she exclaimed 'There! . . . And what's the first thing I do when I come down here?' They had only come last night, driving through June lanes, alone with Bill it was understood, leaving London, sud-denly become dissolute and dirty, to sit down to dinner. 'What do I do? Can I say it aloud? Is it permitted, Mrs Swithin? Yes, everything can be said in this house. I take off my stays' (here she pressed her hands to her sides—she was stout) 'and roll in the grass. Roll—you'll believe that . . .' She laughed wholeheartedly. She had given up dealing with her figure and thus gained freedom.

'That's genuine,' Isa thought. Quite genuine. And her love of the country too. Often when Ralph Manresa had to stay in town she came down alone; wore an old garden hat; taught the village women *not* how to pickle and preserve; but how to weave frivolous baskets out of coloured straw. Pleasure's what they want she said. You often heard her, if you called, yodelling among the hollyhocks 'Hoity te doity te ray do . . .'

A thorough good sort she was. She made old Bart feel young. Out of the corner of his eye, as he raised his glass, he saw a flash of white in the garden. Someone passing.

The scullery maid, before the plates came out, was cooling her cheeks by the lily pond.

There had always been lilies there, self-sown from wind-dropped seed, floating red and white on the green plates of their leaves. Water, for hundreds of years, had silted down into the hollow, and lay there four or five feet deep over a black cushion of mud.

Under the thick plate of green water, glazed in their self-centred world, fish swam—gold, splashed with white, streaked with black or silver. Silently they manœuvred in their water world, poised in the blue patch made by the sky, or shot silently to the edge where the grass, trembling, made a fringe of nodding shadow. On the water-pavement spiders printed their delicate feet. A grain fell and spiralled down; a petal fell, filled and sank. At that the fleet of boat-shaped bodies paused; poised; equipped; mailed; then with a waver of undulation off they flashed.

It was in that deep centre, in that black heart, that the lady had drowned herself. Ten years since the pool had been dredged and a thigh bone recovered. Alas, it was a sheep's, not a lady's. And sheep have no ghosts, for sheep have no souls. But, the servants insisted, they must have a ghost; the ghost must be a lady's, who had drowned herself for love. So none of them would walk by the lily pool at night, only now when the sun shone and the gentry still sat at table.

The flower petal sank; the maid returned to the kitchen; Bartholomew sipped his wine. Happy he felt as a boy; yet reckless as an old man; an unusual; an agreeable sensation. Fumbling in his mind for something to say to the adorable lady, he chose the first thing that came handy; the story of the sheep's thigh.

'Servants', he said, 'must have their ghost.' Kitchen-maids must have their drowned lady.

'But so must I!' cried the wild child of nature, Mrs Manresa. She became, of a sudden, solemn as an owl. She *knew*, she said, pinching a bit of bread to make this emphatic, that Ralph, when he was at the war, couldn't have been killed without her seeing him—'wherever I was, whatever I was doing,' she added, waving her hands so that the diamonds flashed in the sun.

'I don't feel that,' said Mrs Swithin, shaking her head.

'No,' Mrs Manresa laughed. 'You wouldn't. None of you would. You see I'm on a level with . . .' she waited till Candish had retired, 'the servants. I'm nothing like so grown up as you are.'

She preened, approving her adolescence. Rightly or wrongly? A spring of feeling bubbled up through her mud. They had laid theirs with blocks of marble. Sheep's bones were sheep's bones to them, not the relics of the drowned Lady Ermyntrude.

'And which camp', said Bartholomew turning to the unknown guest, 'd'you belong to? The grown, or the ungrown?'

Isabella opened her mouth, hoping that Dodge would open his, and so enable her to place him. But he sat staring. 'I beg your pardon, sir?' he said. They all looked at him. 'I was looking at the pictures.'

[41]

The picture looked at nobody. The picture drew them down the paths of silence.

Lucy broke it.

'Mrs Manresa, I'm going to ask you a favour—If it comes to a pinch this afternoon, will you sing?'

This afternoon? Mrs Manresa was aghast. Was it the pageant? She had never dreamt it was this afternoon. They would never have thrust themselves in— had they known it was this afternoon. And, of course, once more the chime pealed. Isa heard the first chime; and the second; and the third—If it was wet, it would be in the Barn; if it was fine on the terrace. And which would it be, wet or fine? And they all looked out of the window. Then the door opened. Candish said Mr Giles had come. Mr Giles would be down in a moment.

Giles had come. He had seen the great silver-plated car at the door with the initials R. M. twisted so as to look at a distance like a coronet. Visitors, he had concluded, as he drew up behind; and had gone to his room to change. The ghost of convention rose to the surface, as a blush or a tear rises to the surface at the pressure of emotion; so the car touched his training. He must change. And he came into the dining-room looking like a cricketer, in flannels, wearing a blue coat with brass buttons; though he was enraged. Had he not read, in the morning paper, in the train, that sixteen men* had been shot, others prisoned, just over there, across the gulf, in the flat land which divided them from the continent? Yet he changed. It was Aunt Lucy, waving her hand at him as he came in, who made him change. He hung his grievances on her, as one hangs a coat on a hook, instinctively. Aunt Lucy, foolish, free; always, since he had chosen, after leaving college, to take a job in the city, expressing her amazement, her amusement, at men who spent their lives, buying and selling—ploughs? glass beads was it? or stocks and shares?—to savages who wished most oddly—for were they not beautiful naked?—to dress and live like the English? A frivolous, a malignant statement hers was of a problem which, for he had no special gift, no capital, and had been furiously in love with his wife—he nodded to her across the table—had afflicted him for ten years. Given his choice, he would have chosen to farm. But he was not given his choice. So one thing led to another; and the conglomeration of things pressed you flat; held you fast, like a fish in water. So he came for the weekend, and changed.

'How d'you do?' he said all round; nodded to the unknown guest; took against him; and ate his fillet of sole.

He was the very type of all that Mrs Manresa adored. His hair curled; far from running away, as many chins did, his was firm; the nose straight, if short; the eyes, of course, with that hair, blue; and

[43]

finally to make the type complete, there was something fierce, untamed, in the expression which incited her, even at forty-five, to furbish up her ancient batteries.

'He is my husband,' Isabella thought, as they nodded across the bunch of many-coloured flowers. 'The father of my children.' It worked, that old cliché; she felt pride; and affection; then pride again in herself, whom he had chosen. It was a shock to find, after the morning's look in the glass, and the arrow of desire shot through her last night by the gentleman farmer, how much she felt when he came in, not a dapper city gent, but a cricketer, of love; and of hate.

They had met first in Scotland, fishing—she from one rock, he from another. Her line had got tangled; she had given over, and had watched him with the stream rushing between his legs, casting, casting— until, like a thick ingot of silver bent in the middle, the salmon had leapt, had been caught, and she had loved him.

Bartholomew too loved him; and noted his anger— about what? But he remembered his guest. The family was not a family in the presence of strangers. He must, rather laboriously, tell them the story of the pictures at which the unknown guest had been looking when Giles came in.

'That', he indicated the man with the horse, 'was my ancestor. He had a dog. The dog was famous. The dog has his place in history. He left it on record that he wished his dog to be buried with him.'

They looked at the picture.

'I always feel', Lucy broke the silence, 'he's saying: "Paint my dog."'

'But what about the horse?' said Mrs Manresa.

'The horse,' said Bartholomew, putting on his glasses. He looked at the horse. The hindquarters were not satisfactory.

But William Dodge was still looking at the lady.

'Ah,' said Bartholomew who had bought that picture because he liked that picture, 'you're an artist.'

Dodge denied it, for the second time in half an hour, or so Isa noted.

What for did a good sort like the woman Manresa bring these half-breeds in her trail? Giles asked himself. And his silence made its contribution to talk— Dodge that is, shook his head. 'I like that picture.' That was all he could bring himself to say.

'And you're right,' said Bartholomew. 'A man—I forget his name—a man connected with some Institute, a man who goes about giving advice, gratis, to descendants like ourselves, degenerate descendants, said ... said ...' He paused. They all looked at the lady. But she looked over their heads, looking at nothing. She led them down green glades into the heart of silence.

'Said it was by Sir Joshua?'* Mrs Manresa broke the silence abruptly.

'No, no,' William Dodge said hastily, but under his breath.

'Why's he afraid?' Isabella asked herself. A poor specimen he was; afraid to stick up for his own beliefs—just as she was afraid, of her husband. Didn't she write her poetry in a book bound like an account book lest Giles might suspect? She looked at Giles.

He had finished his fish; he had eaten quickly, not to keep them waiting. Now there was cherry tart. Mrs Manresa was counting the stones.

'Tinker, tailor, soldier, sailor, apothecary, plough-boy . . . that's me!' she cried, delighted to have it confirmed by the cherry stones that she was a wild child of nature.

'You believe', said the old gentleman, courteously chaffing her, 'in that too?'

'Of course, of course I do!' she cried. Now she was on the rails again. Now she was a thorough good sort again. And they too were delighted; now they could follow in her wake and leave the silver and dun shades that led to the heart of silence.

'I had a father', said Dodge beneath his breath to Isa who sat next him, 'who loved pictures.'

'Oh, I too!' she exclaimed. Flurriedly, disconnect-edly, she explained. She used to stay when she was a child, when she had the whooping cough, with an uncle, a clergyman; who wore a skull cap; and never did anything; didn't even preach; but made up poems, walking in his garden, saying them aloud.

'People thought him mad,' she said. 'I didn't . . .'
She stopped.

'Tinker, tailor, soldier, sailor, apothecary, plough-
boy . . . It appears', said old Bartholomew, laying
down his spoon, 'that I am a thief. Shall we take our
coffee in the garden?' He rose.

Isa dragged her chair across the gravel, muttering:
'To what dark antre of the unvisited earth, or wind-
brushed forest, shall we go now? Or spin from star
to star and dance in the maze of the moon? Or . . .'

She held her deck-chair at the wrong angle. The
frame with the notches was upside down.

'Songs my uncle taught me?' said William Dodge,
hearing her mutter. He unfolded the chair and fixed
the bar into the right notch.

She flushed, as if she had spoken in an empty room
and someone had stepped out from behind a curtain.

'Don't you, if you're doing something with your
hands, talk nonsense?' she stumbled. But what did he
do with his hands, the white, the fine, the shapely?

Giles went back to the house and brought more chairs
and placed them in a semi-circle, so that the view
might be shared, and the shelter of the old wall. For
by some lucky chance a wall had been built continuing the house, it might be with the intention of adding
another wing, on the raised ground in the sun. But
funds were lacking; the plan was abandoned, and the

[47]

wall remained, nothing but a wall. Later, another generation had planted fruit trees, which in time had spread their arms widely across the red orange weathered brick. Mrs Sands called it a good year if she could make six pots of apricot jam from them—the fruit was never sweet enough for dessert. Perhaps three apricots were worth enclosing in muslin bags. But they were so beautiful, naked, with one flushed cheek, one green, that Mrs Swithin left them naked, and the wasps burrowed holes.

The ground sloped up, so that to quote Figgis's Guide Book* (1833), 'it commanded a fine view over the surrounding country ... The spire of Bolney Minster, Rough Norton woods, and on an eminence rather to the left, Hogben's Folly, so called because ...'

The Guide Book still told the truth. 1833 was true in 1939. No house had been built; no town had sprung up. Hogben's Folly was still eminent; the very flat, field-parcelled land had changed only in this— the tractor had to some extent superseded the plough. The horse had gone; but the cow remained. If Figgis were here now, Figgis would have said the same. So they always said when in summer they sat there to drink coffee, if they had guests. When they were alone, they said nothing. They looked at the view; they looked at what they knew, to see if what they knew might perhaps be different today. Most days it was the same.

'That's what makes a view so sad,' said Mrs Swithin, lowering herself into the deck-chair which Giles had brought her. 'And so beautiful. It'll be there', she nodded at the strip of gauze laid upon the distant fields, 'when we're not.'

Giles nicked his chair into position with a jerk. Thus only could he show his irritation, his rage with old fogies who sat and looked at views over coffee and cream when the whole of Europe—over there—was bristling like . . . He had no command of metaphor. Only the ineffective word 'hedgehog' illustrated his vision of Europe, bristling with guns, poised with planes. At any moment guns would rake that land into furrows; planes splinter Bolney Minster into smithereens and blast the Folly. He, too, loved the view and blamed Aunt Lucy, looking at views, instead of—doing what? What she had done was to marry a squire now dead; she had borne two children, one in Canada, the other, married, in Birmingham. His father, whom he loved, he exempted from censure; as for himself, one thing followed another; and so he sat, with old fogies, looking at views.

'Beautiful,' said Mrs Manresa, 'beautiful . . .' she mumbled. She was lighting a cigarette. The breeze blew out her match. Giles hollowed his hand and lit another. She too was exempted—why, he could not say.

'Since you're interested in pictures,' said Bartholomew, turning to the silent guest, 'why, tell me, are we, as a race, so incurious, irresponsive and insensitive'—the champagne had given him a flow of unusual three-decker words—'to that noble art, whereas, Mrs Manresa, if she'll allow me my old man's liberty, has her Shakespeare by heart?'

'Shakespeare by heart!' Mrs Manresa protested. She struck an attitude. 'To be, or not to be, that is the question. Whether 'tis nobler . . . Go on!' she nudged Giles, who sat next her.

'Fade far away and quite forget what thou amongst the leaves hast never known . . .' Isa supplied the first words that came into her head by way of helping her husband out of his daily difficulty.

'The weariness, the torture, and the fret . . .'* William Dodge added, burying the end of his cigarette in a grave between two stones.

'There!' Bartholomew exclaimed, cocking his forefinger aloft. 'That proves it! What springs touched, what secret drawer displays its treasures, if I say'— he raised more fingers—'Reynolds! Constable!* Crome!'*

'Why called "Old"?' Mrs Manresa thrust in.

'We haven't the words—we haven't the words,' Mrs Swithin protested. 'Behind the eyes; not on the lips; that's all.'

'Thoughts without words,' her brother mused. 'Can that be?'

'Quite beyond me!' cried Mrs Manresa, shaking her head. 'Much too clever! May I help myself? I know it's wrong. But I've reached the age—and the figure—when I do what I like.'

She took the little silver cream jug and let the smooth fluid curl luxuriously into her coffee, to which she added a shovel full of brown sugar candy. Sensuously, rhythmically, she stirred the mixture round and round.

'Take what you like! Help yourself!' Bartholomew exclaimed. He felt the champagne withdrawing and hastened, before the last trace of geniality was withdrawn, to make the most of it, as if he cast one last look into a lit-up chamber before going to bed.

The wild child, afloat once more on the tide of the old man's benignity, looked over her coffee cup at Giles, with whom she felt in conspiracy. A thread united them—visible, invisible, like those threads, now seen, now not, that unite trembling grass blades in autumn before the sun rises. She had met him once only, at a cricket match. And then had been spun between them an early morning thread before the twigs and leaves of real friendship emerge. She looked before she drank. Looking was part of drinking. Why waste sensation, she seemed to ask, why waste a single drop that can be pressed out of this ripe, this melting, this adorable world? Then she drank. And the air round her became threaded with sensation. Bartholomew felt it; Giles felt it. Had he been a horse, the thin brown skin would have twitched, as if

a fly had settled. Isabella twitched too. Jealousy, anger
pierced her skin.

'And now,' said Mrs Manresa, putting down her
cup, 'about this entertainment—this pageant, into
which we've gone and butted'—she made it, too,
seem ripe like the apricot into which the wasps were
burrowing—'Tell me, what's it to be?' She turned.
'Don't I hear?' She listened. She heard laughter, down
among the bushes, where the terrace dipped to the
bushes.

Beyond the lily pool the ground sank again, and in
that dip of the ground, bushes and brambles had
mobbed themselves together. It was always shady;
sun-flecked in summer, dark and damp in winter. In
the summer there were always butterflies; fritillaries
darting through; Red Admirals feasting and floating;
cabbage whites, unambitiously fluttering round a
bush, like muslin milkmaids, content to spend a life
there. Butterfly catching, for generation after generation, began there; for Bartholomew and Lucy; for
Giles; for George it had begun only the day before
yesterday, when, in his little green net, he had caught
a cabbage white.

It was the very place for a dressing-room, just as,
obviously, the terrace was the very place for a
play.

'The very place!' Miss La Trobe had exclaimed the

first time she came to call and was shown the grounds.
It was a winter's day. The trees were leafless then.

'That's the place for a pageant, Mr Oliver!' she had
exclaimed. 'Winding in and out between the trees . . .'
She waved her hand at the trees standing bare in the
clear light of January.

'There the stage; here the audience; and down there
among the bushes a perfect dressing-room for the
actors.'

She was always all agog to get things up. But where
did she spring from? With that name she wasn't
presumably pure English. From the Channel Islands
perhaps? Only her eyes and something about her
always made Mrs Bingham suspect that she had
Russian blood in her. 'Those deep-set eyes; that very
square jaw' reminded her—not that she had been to
Russia—of the Tartars. Rumour said that she had
kept a tea shop at Winchester; that had failed. She
had been an actress. That had failed. She had bought
a four-roomed cottage and shared it with an actress.
They had quarrelled. Very little was actually known
about her. Outwardly she was swarthy, sturdy and
thick set; strode about the fields in a smock frock;
sometimes with a cigarette in her mouth; often with a
whip in her hand; and used rather strong language—
perhaps, then, she wasn't altogether a lady? At any
rate, she had a passion for getting things up.

*

The laughter died away.

'Are they going to act?' Mrs Manresa asked.

'Act; dance; sing; a little bit of everything,' said Giles.

'Miss La Trobe is a lady of wonderful energy,' said Mrs Swithin.

'She makes everyone do something,' said Isabella.

'Our part', said Bartholomew, 'is to be the audience. And a very important part too.'

'Also, we provide the tea,' said Mrs Swithin.

'Shan't we go and help?' said Mrs Manresa. 'Cut up bread and butter?'

'No, no,' said Mr Oliver. 'We are the audience.'

'One year we had *Gammer Gurton's Needle*,'* said Mrs Swithin. 'One year we wrote the play ourselves. The son of our blacksmith—Tony? Tommy?—had the loveliest voice. And Elsie at the Crossways—how she mimicked! Took us all off. Bart; Giles; Old Flimsy—that's me. People are gifted—very. The question is—how to bring it out? That's where she's so clever—Miss La Trobe. Of course, there's the whole of English literature to choose from. But how can one choose? Often on a wet day I begin counting up; what I've read; what I haven't read.'

'And leaving books on the floor,' said her brother. 'Like the pig in the story; or was it a donkey?'

She laughed, tapping him lightly on the knee.

'The donkey who couldn't choose between hay and

turnips and so starved,' Isabella explained, interpos-
ing—anything—between her aunt and her husband,
who hated this kind of talk this afternoon. Books
open; no conclusion come to; and he sitting in the
audience.

'We remain seated'—'We are the audience.' Words
this afternoon ceased to lie flat in the sentence. They
rose, became menacing and shook their fists at you.
This afternoon he wasn't Giles Oliver come to see the
villagers act their annual pageant; manacled to a rock
he was, and forced passively to behold indescribable
horror. His face showed it; and Isa, not knowing
what to say, abruptly, half purposely, knocked over a
coffee cup.

William Dodge caught it as it fell. He held it for a
moment. He turned it. From the faint blue mark, as
of crossed daggers, in the glaze at the bottom he knew
that it was English, made perhaps at Nottingham;
date about 1760. His expression, considering the
daggers, coming to this conclusion, gave Giles
another peg on which to hang his rage as one hangs a
coat on a peg, conveniently. A toady; a lickspittle;
not a downright plain man of his senses; but a teaser
and twitcher; a fingerer of sensations; picking and
choosing; dillying and dallying; not a man to have
straightforward love for a woman—his head was
close to Isa's head—but simply a——At this word,
which he could not speak in public, he pursed his
lips; and the signet-ring on his little finger looked

redder, for the flesh next it whitened as he gripped the arm of his chair.

'Oh what fun!' cried Mrs Manresa in her fluty voice. 'A little bit of everything. A song; a dance; then a play acted by the villagers themselves. Only,' here she turned with her head on one side to Isabella, 'I'm sure *she's* written it. Haven't you, Mrs Giles?'

Isa flushed and denied it.

'For myself,' Mrs Manresa continued, 'speaking plainly, I can't put two words together. I don't know how it is—such a chatterbox as I am with my tongue, once I hold a pen——' She made a face, screwed her fingers as if she held a pen in them. But the pen she held thus on the little table absolutely refused to move.

'And my handwriting—so huge—so clumsy—' She made another face and dropped the invisible pen.

Very delicately William Dodge set the cup in its saucer. 'Now *he*', said Mrs Manresa, as if referring to the delicacy with which he did this, and imputing to him the same skill in writing, 'writes beautifully. Every letter perfectly formed.'

Again they all looked at him. Instantly he put his hands in his pockets.

Isabella guessed the word that Giles had not spoken. Well, was it wrong if he was that word? Why judge each other? Do we know each other? Not here, not now. But somewhere, this cloud, this crust, this doubt, this dust——She waited for a rhyme, it failed her; but somewhere surely one sun would shine and all, without a doubt, would be clear.

She started. Again, sounds of laughter reached her.

'I think I hear them,' she said. 'They're getting ready. They're dressing up in the bushes.'

Miss La Trobe was pacing to and fro between the leaning birch trees. One hand was deep stuck in her jacket pocket; the other held a foolscap sheet. She was reading what was written there. She had the look of a commander pacing his deck. The leaning graceful trees with black bracelets circling the silver bark were distant about a ship's length.

Wet would it be, or fine? Out came the sun; and, shading her eyes in the attitude proper to an Admiral on his quarter-deck, she decided to risk the engagement out of doors. Doubts were over. All stage properties, she commanded, must be moved from the Barn to the bushes. It was done. And the actors, while she paced, taking all responsibility and plumping for fine, not wet, dressed among the brambles. Hence the laughter.

The clothes were strewn on the grass. Cardboard crowns, swords made of silver paper, turbans that were sixpenny dish cloths, lay on the grass or were flung on the bushes. There were pools of red and purple in the shade; flashes of silver in the sun. The dresses attracted the butterflies. Red and silver, blue and yellow gave off warmth and sweetness. Red Admirals gluttonously absorbed richness from dish cloths, cabbage whites drank icy coolness from silver paper. Flitting, tasting, returning, they sampled the colours.

Miss La Trobe stopped her pacing and surveyed the scene. 'It has the makings . . .' she murmured. For another play always lay behind the play she had just written. Shading her eyes, she looked. The butterflies circling; the light changing; the children leaping; the mothers laughing——'No, I don't get it,' she muttered and resumed her pacing.

'Bossy' they called her privately, just as they called Mrs Swithin 'Flimsy'. Her abrupt manner and stocky figure; her thick ankles and sturdy shoes; her rapid decisions barked out in guttural accents—all this 'got their goat'. No one liked to be ordered about singly. But in little troops they appealed to her. Someone must lead. Then too they could put the blame on her. Suppose it poured?

'Miss La Trobe!' they hailed her now. 'What's the idea about this?'

She stopped. David and Iris each had a hand on the gramophone. It must be hidden; yet must be close enough to the audience to be heard. Well, hadn't she given orders? Where were the hurdles covered in leaves? Fetch them. Mr Streatfield had said he would

see to it. Where was Mr Streatfield? No clergyman
was visible. Perhaps he's in the Barn? 'Tommy, cut
along and fetch him.' 'Tommy's wanted in the first
scene.' 'Beryl then . . .' The mothers disputed. One
child had been chosen; another not. Fair hair was
unjustly preferred to dark. Mrs Ebury had forbidden
Fanny to act because of the nettle-rash. There was
another name in the village for nettle-rash.

Mrs Ball's cottage was not what you might call
clean. In the last war Mrs Ball lived with another man
while her husband was in the trenches. All this Miss
La Trobe knew, but refused to be mixed up in it. She
splashed into the fine mesh like a great stone into the
lily pool. The criss-cross was shattered. Only the
roots beneath water were of use to her. Vanity, for
example, made them all malleable. The boys wanted
the big parts; the girls wanted the fine clothes.
Expenses had to be kept down. Ten pounds was the
limit. Thus conventions were outraged. Swathed in
conventions, they couldn't see, as she could, that a
dish cloth wound round a head in the open looked
much richer than real silk. So they squabbled; but she
kept out of it. Waiting for Mr Streatfield, she paced
between the birch trees.

The other trees were magnificently straight. They
were not too regular; but regular enough to suggest
columns in a church; in a church without a roof;
in an open-air cathedral, a place where swallows
darting seemed, by the regularity of the trees, to make

a pattern, dancing, like the Russians, only not to music, but to the unheard rhythm of their own wild hearts.

The laughter died away.

'We must possess our souls in patience,' said Mrs Manresa again. 'Or could we help?' she suggested, glancing over her shoulder, 'with those chairs?'

Candish, a gardener, and a maid were all bringing chairs—for the audience. There was nothing for the audience to do. Mrs Manresa suppressed a yawn. They were silent. They stared at the view, as if something might happen in one of those fields to relieve them of the intolerable burden of remaining silent, doing nothing, in company. Their minds and bodies were too close, yet not close enough. We aren't free, each of them felt separately, to feel or think separately, nor yet to fall asleep. We're too close; but not close enough. So they fidgeted.

The heat had increased. The clouds had vanished. All was sun now. The view laid bare by the sun was flattened, silenced, stilled. The cows were motionless; the brick wall, no longer sheltering, beat back grains of heat. Old Mr Oliver sighed profoundly. His head jerked; his hand fell. It fell within an inch of the dog's head on the grass by his side. Then up he jerked it again on to his knee.

Giles glared. With his hands bound tight round his

knees he stared at the flat fields. Staring, glaring, he sat silent.

Isabella felt prisoned. Through the bars of the prison, through the sleep haze that deflected them, blunt arrows bruised her; of love, then of hate. Through other people's bodies she felt neither love nor hate distinctly. Most consciously she felt—she had drunk sweet wine at luncheon—a desire for water. 'A beaker of cold water, a beaker of cold water,' she repeated, and saw water surrounded by walls of shining glass.

Mrs Manresa longed to relax and curl in a corner with a cushion, a picture paper, and a bag of sweets.

Mrs Swithin and William surveyed the view aloofly, and with detachment.

How tempting, how very tempting, to let the view triumph; to reflect its ripple; to let their own minds ripple; to let outlines elongate and pitch over—so—with a sudden jerk.

Mrs Manresa yielded, pitched, plunged, then pulled herself up.

'What a view!' she exclaimed, pretending to dust the ashes of her cigarette, but in truth concealing her yawn. Then she sighed, pretending to express not her own drowsiness, but something connected with what she felt about views.

Nobody answered her. The flat fields glared green yellow, blue yellow, red yellow, then blue again. The repetition was senseless, hideous, stupefying.

'Then,' said Mrs Swithin, in a low voice, as if the exact moment for speech had come, as if she had promised, and it was time to fulfil her promise, 'come, come and I'll show you the house.'

She addressed no one in particular. But William Dodge knew she meant him. He rose with a jerk, like a toy suddenly pulled straight by a string.

'What energy!' Mrs Manresa half sighed, half yawned. 'Have I the courage to go too?' Isabella asked herself. They were going; above all things, she desired cold water, a beaker of cold water; but desire petered out, suppressed by the leaden duty she owed to others. She watched them go—Mrs Swithin tottering yet tripping; and Dodge unfurled and straightened, as he strode beside her along the blazing tiles under the hot wall, till they reached the shade of the house.

A match-box fell—Bartholomew's. His fingers had loosed it; he had dropped it. He gave up the game; he couldn't be bothered. With his head on one side, his hand dangling above the dog's head, he slept; he snored.

Mrs Swithin paused for a moment in the hall among the gilt-clawed tables.

'This', she said, 'is the staircase. And now—up we go.'

She went up, two stairs ahead of her guest. Lengths

of yellow satin unfurled themselves on a cracked canvas as they mounted.

'Not an ancestress,' said Mrs Swithin, as they came level with the head in the picture. 'But we claim her because we've known her—O, ever so many years. Who was she?' she gazed. 'Who painted her?' She shook her head. She looked lit up, as if for a banquet, with the sun pouring over her.

'But I like her best in the moonlight,' Mrs Swithin reflected, and mounted more stairs.

She panted slightly, going upstairs. Then she ran her hands over the sunk books in the wall on the landing, as if they were pan pipes.

'Here are the poets from whom we descend by way of the mind, Mr . . .' she murmured. She had forgotten his name. Yet she had singled him out.

'My brother says, they built the house north for shelter, not south for sun. So they're damp in the winter.' She paused. 'And now what comes next?'

She stopped. There was a door.

'The morning room.' She opened the door. 'Where my mother received her guests.'

Two chairs faced each other on either side of a fine fluted mantelpiece. He looked over her shoulder.

She shut the door.

'Now up, now up again.' Again they mounted. 'Up and up they went,' she panted, seeing, it seemed, an invisible procession, 'up and up to bed.'

'A bishop; a traveller;—I've forgotten even their names. I ignore. I forget.'

She stopped at a window in the passage and held back the curtain. Beneath was the garden, bathed in sun. The grass was sleek and shining. Three white pigeons were flirting and tiptoeing as ornate as ladies in ball dresses. Their elegant bodies swayed as they minced with tiny steps on their little pink feet upon the grass. Suddenly, up they rose in a flutter, circled, and flew away.

'Now,' she said, 'for the bedrooms.' She tapped twice very distinctly on a door. With her head on one side, she listened.

'One never knows', she murmured, 'if there's somebody there.' Then she flung open the door.

He half expected to see somebody there, naked, or half dressed, or knelt in prayer. But the room was empty. The room was tidy as a pin, not slept in for months, a spare room. Candles stood on the dressing-table. The counterpane was straight. Mrs Swithin stopped by the bed.

'Here,' she said, 'yes, here,' she tapped the counter-pane, 'I was born. In this bed.'

Her voice died away. She sank down on the edge of the bed. She was tired, no doubt, by the stairs, by the heat.

'But we have other lives, I think, I hope,' she murmured. 'We live in others, Mr ... We live in things.'

She spoke simply. She spoke with an effort. She spoke as if she must overcome her tiredness out of charity towards a stranger, a guest. She had forgotten his name. Twice she had said 'Mr' and stopped.

The furniture was mid-Victorian, bought at Maples,* perhaps, in the forties. The carpet was covered with small purple dots. And a white circle marked the place where the slop pail had stood by the washstand.

Could he say 'I'm William'? He wished to. Old and frail she had climbed the stairs. She had spoken her thoughts, ignoring, not caring if he thought her, as he had, inconsequent, sentimental, foolish. She had lent him a hand to help him up a steep place. She had guessed his trouble. Sitting on the bed he heard her sing, swinging her little legs, 'Come and see my sea weeds, come and see my sea shells, come and see my dicky bird hop upon its perch'—an old child's nursery rhyme to help a child. Standing by the cupboard in the corner he saw her reflected in the glass. Cut off from their bodies, their eyes smiled, their bodiless eyes, at their eyes in the glass.

Then she slipped off the bed.

'Now,' she said, 'what comes next?' and pattered down the corridor. A door stood open. Everyone was out in the garden. The room was like a ship deserted by its crew. The children had been playing—there was a spotted horse in the middle of the carpet. The nurse had been sewing—there was a piece of linen on

[65]

the table. The baby had been in the cot. The cot was empty.

'The nursery,' said Mrs Swithin.

Words raised themselves and became symbolical. 'The cradle of our race,' she seemed to say.

Dodge crossed to the fireplace and looked at the Newfoundland Dog in the Christmas Annual that was pinned to the wall. The room smelt warm and sweet; of clothes drying; of milk; of biscuits and warm water. 'Good Friends' the picture was called. A rushing sound came in through the open door. He turned. The old woman had wandered out into the passage and leant against the window.

He left the door open for the crew to come back to and joined her.

Down in the courtyard beneath the window cars were assembling. Their narrow black roofs were laid together like the blocks of a floor. Chauffeurs were jumping down; here old ladies gingerly advanced black legs with silver-buckled shoes; old men striped trousers. Young men in shorts leapt out on one side; girls with skin-coloured legs on the other. There was a purring and a churning of the yellow gravel. The audience was assembling. But they, looking down from the window, were truants, detached. Together they leant half out of the window.

And then a breeze blew and all the muslin blinds fluttered out, as if some majestic goddess, rising from her throne among her peers, had tossed her amber-

coloured raiment, and the other gods, seeing her rise
and go, laughed, and their laughter floated her on.

Mrs Swithin put her hands to her hair, for the
breeze had ruffled it.

'Mr . . .' she began.

'I'm William,' he interrupted.

At that she smiled a ravishing girl's smile, as if the
wind had warmed the wintry blue in her eyes to
amber.

'I took you', she apologized, 'away from your
friends, William, because I felt wound tight here . . .'
She touched her bony forehead upon which a blue
vein wriggled like a blue worm. But her eyes in their
caves of bone were still lambent. He saw her eyes
only. And he wished to kneel before her, to kiss her
hand, and to say: 'At school they held me under a
bucket of dirty water, Mrs Swithin; when I looked
up, the world was dirty, Mrs Swithin; so I married;
but my child's not my child, Mrs Swithin. I'm a half-
man, Mrs Swithin; a flickering, mind-divided little
snake in the grass, Mrs Swithin; as Giles saw; but
you've healed me . . .' So he wished to say; but said
nothing; and the breeze went lolloping along the
corridors, blowing the blinds out.

Once more he looked and she looked down on to
the yellow gravel that made a crescent round the
door. Pendant from her chain her cross swung as she
leant out and the sun struck it. How could she weight
herself down by that sleek symbol? How stamp

herself, so volatile, so vagrant, with that image? As he looked at it, they were truants no more. The purring of the wheels became vocal. 'Hurry, hurry, hurry,' it seemed to say, 'or you'll be late. Hurry, hurry, hurry, or the best seats'll be taken.'

'O,' cried Mrs Swithin, 'there's Mr Streatfield!' And they saw a clergyman, a strapping clergyman, carrying a hurdle, a leafy hurdle. He was striding through the cars with the air of a person of authority, who is awaited, expected, and now comes.

'Is it time,' said Mrs Swithin, 'to go and join——' She left the sentence unfinished, as if she were of two minds, and they fluttered to right and to left, like pigeons rising from the grass.

The audience was assembling. They came streaming along the paths and spreading across the lawn. Some were old; some were in the prime of life. There were children among them. Among them, as Mr Figgis might have observed, were representatives of our most respected families—the Dyces of Denton; the Wickhams of Owlswick; and so on. Some had been there for centuries, never selling an acre. On the other hand there were new-comers, the Manresas, bringing the old houses up to date, adding bathrooms. And a scatter of odds and ends, like Cobbet of Cobbs Corner, retired, it was understood, on a pension from a tea plantation. Not an asset. He did his own housework and dug in his garden. The building of a car factory and of an aerodrome in the neighbourhood had attracted a number of unattached floating residents. Also there was Mr Page, the reporter, representing the local paper. Roughly speaking, however, had Figgis been there in person and called a roll call, half the ladies and gentlemen present would have said: '*Adsum*;* I'm here, in place of my grandfather or great-grandfather,' as the case might be. At this very moment, half-past three on a June day in 1939 they greeted each other, and as they took their seats, finding if possible a seat next one another, they said: 'That hideous new house at Pyes Corner! What an eyesore! And those bungalows!—have you seen 'em?'

Again, had Figgis called the names of the villagers, they too would have answered. Mrs Sands was born Iliffe; Candish's mother was one of the Perrys. The green mounds in the churchyard had been cast up by their molings, which for centuries had made the earth friable. True, there were absentees when Mr Streatfield called his roll call in the church. The motor bike, the motor bus, and the movies—when Mr Streatfield called his roll call, he laid the blame on them.

Rows of chairs, deck-chairs, gilt chairs, hired cane chairs, and indigenous garden seats had been drawn up on the terrace. There were plenty of seats for everybody. But some preferred to sit on the ground. Certainly Miss La Trobe had spoken the truth when she said: 'The very place for a pageant!' The lawn was as flat as the floor of a theatre. The terrace, rising, made a natural stage. The trees barred the stage like pillars. And the human figure was seen to great advantage against a background of sky. As for the weather, it was turning out, against all expectation, a very fine day. A perfect summer afternoon.

'What luck!' Mrs Carter was saying. 'Last year . . .' Then the play began. Was it, or was it not, the play? Chuff, chuff, chuff sounded from the bushes. It was the noise a machine makes when something has gone wrong. Some sat down hastily; others stopped talking guiltily. All looked at the bushes. For the stage was empty. Chuff, chuff, chuff the machine buzzed in the bushes. While they looked apprehensively and some finished their sentences, a small girl, like a rosebud in pink, advanced; took her stand on a mat, behind a conch, hung with leaves and piped:

Gentles and simples, I address you all . . .

So it was the play then. Or was it the prologue?

Come hither for our festival (she continued)
This is a pageant, all may see
Drawn from our island history.
England am I . . .

'She's England,' they whispered. 'It's begun.' 'The prologue,' they added, looking down at the programme.

'*England am I,*' she piped again; and stopped.
She had forgotten her lines.

'Hear! Hear!' said an old man in a white waistcoat briskly. 'Bravo! Bravo!'

'Blast 'em!' cursed Miss La Trobe, hidden behind the tree. She looked along the front row. They glared as if they were exposed to a frost that nipped them and fixed them all at the same level. Only Bond the cowman looked fluid and natural.

'Music!' she signalled. 'Music!' But the machine continued: Chuff, chuff, chuff.

'*A child new born . . .*' she prompted.

'*A child new born,*' Phyllis Jones continued,

Sprung from the sea
Whose billows blown by mighty storm
Cut off from France and Germany
    This isle.

She glanced back over her shoulder. Chuff, chuff, chuff, the machine buzzed. A long line of villagers in shirts made of sacking began passing in and out in single file behind her between the trees. They were singing, but not a word reached the audience.

England am I, Phyllis continued, facing the audience.

Now weak and small
A child, as all may see . . .

Her words peppered the audience as with a shower of hard little stones. Mrs Manresa in the very centre smiled; but she felt as if her skin cracked when she smiled. There was a vast vacancy between her, the singing villagers and the piping child.

[71]

Chuff, chuff, chuff, went the machine like a corn-cutter on a hot day.

The villagers were singing, but half their words were blown away.

Cutting the roads . . . up to the hill top . . . we climbed.
Down in the valley . . . sow, wild boar, hog, rhinoceros,
reindeer . . . Dug ourselves in to the hill top . . . Ground
roots between stones . . . Ground corn . . . till we too . . .
lay under g—r—o—u—n—d . . .

The words petered away. Chuff, chuff, chuff, the machine ticked. Then at last the machine ground out a tune!

Armed against fate
The valiant Rhoderick
Armed and valiant
Bold and blatant
Firm elatant
See the warriors—here they come . . .

The pompous popular tune brayed and blared. Miss La Trobe watched from behind the tree. Muscles loosened; ice cracked. The stout lady in the middle began to beat time with her hand on her chair. Mrs Manresa was humming:

My home is at Windsor, close to the Inn.
Royal George is the name of the pub.
And boys you'll believe me,
I don't want no asking . . .

She was afloat on the stream of the melody. Radiating royalty, complacency, good humour, the wild child was Queen of the festival. The play had begun.

But there was an interruption. 'O,' Miss La Trobe growled behind her tree, 'the torture of these interruptions!'

'Sorry I'm so late,' said Mrs Swithin. She pushed her way through the chairs to a seat beside her brother.

'What's it all about? I've missed the prologue. England? That little girl? Now she's gone . . .'

Phyllis had slipped off her mat.

'And who's this?' asked Mrs Swithin.

It was Hilda, the carpenter's daughter. She now stood where England had stood.

'O, *England's grown* . . .' Miss La Trobe prompted her.

'O, *England's grown a girl now*,' Hilda sang out ('What a lovely voice!' someone exclaimed)

With roses in her hair,
Wild roses, red roses,
She roams the lanes and chooses
A garland for her hair.

'A cushion? Thank you so much,' said Mrs Swithin, stuffing the cushion behind her back. Then she leant forward.

'That's England in the time of Chaucer, I take it. She's been maying, nutting. She has flowers in her hair ... But those passing behind her——' she pointed. 'The Canterbury pilgrims? Look!'

All the time the villagers were passing in and out between the trees. They were singing; but only a word or two was audible '... *wore ruts in the grass ... built the house in the lane* ...' The wind blew away the connecting words of their chant, and then, as they reached the tree at the end they sang:

'*To the shrine of the Saint—to the tomb ... lovers ... believers ... we come...*'

They grouped themselves together.

Then there was a rustle and an interruption. Chairs were drawn back. Isa looked behind her. Mr and Mrs Rupert Haines, detained by a breakdown on the road, had arrived. He was sitting on the right, several rows back, the man in grey.

Meanwhile the pilgrims, having done their homage to the tomb, were, it appeared, tossing hay on their rakes.

> *I kissed a girl and let her go,*
> *Another did I tumble,*
> *In the straw and in the hay ...*

—that was what they were singing, as they scooped and tossed the invisible hay, when she looked round again.

'Scenes from English history,' Mrs Manresa explained to Mrs Swithin. She spoke in a loud cheerful voice, as if the old lady were deaf. 'Merry England.'

She clapped energetically.

The singers scampered away into the bushes. The tune stopped. Chuff, chuff, chuff, the machine ticked. Mrs Manresa looked at her programme. It would take till midnight unless they skipped. Early Briton; Plantagenets; Tudors; Stuarts—she ticked them off, but probably she had forgotten a reign or two.

'Ambitious, ain't it?' she said to Bartholomew, while they waited. Chuff, chuff, chuff went the machine. Could they talk? Could they move? No, for the play was going on. Yet the stage was empty; only the cows moved in the meadows; only the tick of the gramophone needle was heard. The tick, tick, tick seemed to hold them together, tranced. Nothing whatsoever appeared on the stage.

'I'd no notion we looked so nice,' Mrs Swithin whispered to William. Hadn't she? The children; the pilgrims; behind the pilgrims the trees and behind them the fields—the beauty of the visible world took his breath away. Tick, tick, tick the machine continued.

'Marking time,' said old Oliver beneath his breath.

'Which don't exist for us,' Lucy murmured. 'We've only the present.'

'Isn't that enough?' William asked himself. Beauty—isn't that enough? But here Isa fidgeted. Her bare brown arms went nervously to her head. She half turned in her seat. 'No, not for us, who've the future,' she seemed to say. The future disturbing our present. Who was she looking for? William, turning, following her eyes, saw only a man in grey.

The ticking stopped. A dance tune was put on the machine. In time to it, Isa hummed: 'What do I ask? To fly away, from night and day, and issue where— no partings are—but eye meets eye—and . . . O,' she cried aloud: 'Look at her!'

Everyone was clapping and laughing. From behind the bushes issued Queen Elizabeth—Eliza Clark, licensed to sell tobacco. Could she be Mrs Clark of the village shop? She was splendidly made up. Her head, pearl-hung, rose from a vast ruff. Shiny satins draped her. Sixpenny brooches glared like cats' eyes and tigers' eyes; pearls looked down; her cape was made of cloth of silver—in fact swabs used to scour saucepans. She looked the age in person. And when she mounted the soap box in the centre, representing perhaps a rock in the ocean, her size made her appear gigantic. She could reach a flitch of bacon or haul a tub of oil with one sweep of her arm in the shop. For a moment she stood there, eminent, dominant, on the soap box with the blue and sailing clouds behind her. The breeze had risen.

The Queen of this great land . . .
—those were the first words that could be heard above the roar of laughter and applause.

Mistress of ships and bearded men (she bawled)
*Hawkins, Frobisher, Drake,**

[76]

Tumbling their oranges, ingots of silver,
Cargoes of diamonds, ducats of gold,
Down on the jetty, there in the west land,—
(she pointed her fist at the blazing blue sky)
Mistress of pinnacles, spires and palaces—
(her arm swept towards the house)
For me Shakespeare sang—
(a cow mooed. A bird twittered)
The throstle, the mavis (she continued)
In the green wood, the wild wood,
Carolled and sang, praising England, the Queen,
Then there was heard too
On granite and cobble
From Windsor to Oxford
Loud laughter, low laughter
Of warrior and lover,
The fighter, the singer.
The ashen haired babe
(she stretched out her swarthy, muscular arm)
Stretched his arm in contentment
As home from the Isles came
The sea faring men . . .

Here the wind gave a tug at her head dress. Loops of pearls made it top-heavy. She had to steady the ruffle which threatened to blow away.

'Laughter, loud laughter,' Giles muttered. The tune on the gramophone reeled from side to side as if drunk with merriment. Mrs Manresa began beating her foot and humming in time to it.

'Bravo! Bravo!' she cried. 'There's life in the old dog yet!' And she trolloped out the words of the song

with an abandonment which, if vulgar, was a great
help to the Elizabethan age. For the ruff had become
unpinned and great Eliza had forgotten her lines. But
the audience laughed so loud that it did not matter.

'I fear I am not in my perfect mind,'* Giles
muttered to the same tune. Words came to the
surface—he remembered 'a stricken deer in whose
lean flank the world's harsh scorn has struck its thorn
... Exiled from its festival, the music turned ironical
... A churchyard haunter at whom the owl hoots
and the ivy mocks tap-tap-tapping on the pane ...
For they are dead, and I ... I ... I,' he repeated,
forgetting the words, and glaring at his Aunt Lucy
who sat craned forward, her mouth gaping, and her
bony little hands clapping.

What were they laughing at?

At Albert, the village idiot, apparently. There was
no need to dress him up. There he came, acting his
part to perfection. He came ambling across the grass,
mopping and mowing.

I know where the tit nests, he began
In the hedgerow. I know, I know—
What don't I know?
All your secrets, ladies,
And yours too, gentlemen ...

He skipped along the front row of the audience,
leering at each in turn. Now he was picking and
plucking at Great Eliza's skirts. She cuffed him on

the ear. He tweaked her back. He was enjoying himself immensely

'Albert having the time of his life,' Bartholomew muttered.

'Hope he don't have a fit,' Lucy murmured.

'*I know . . . I know . . .*' Albert tittered, skipping round the soap box.

'The village idiot,' whispered a stout black lady— Mrs Elmhurst—who came from a village ten miles distant where they, too, had an idiot. It wasn't nice. Suppose he suddenly did something dreadful? There he was pinching the Queen's skirts. She half covered her eyes, in case he did do—something dreadful.

> *Hoppety, jiggety*, Albert resumed,
> *In at the window, out at the door,*
> *What does the little bird hear?* (he whistled on his fingers.)
> *And see! There's a mouse . . .*
> (he made as if chasing it through the grass)
> *Now the clock strikes!*
> (he stood erect, puffing out his cheeks as if he were blowing a dandelion clock)
> *One, two, three, four . . .*

And off he skipped, as if his turn was over.

'Glad that's over,' said Mrs Elmhurst, uncovering her face. 'Now what comes next? A tableau . . .?'

For helpers, issuing swiftly from the bushes, carrying hurdles, had enclosed the Queen's throne with screens papered to represent walls. They had strewn the ground with rushes. And the pilgrims who had continued their march and their chant in the background, now gathered round the figure of Eliza on her soap box as if to form the audience at a play.

Were they about to act a play in the presence of Queen Elizabeth? Was this, perhaps, the Globe theatre?*

'What does the programme say?' Mrs Herbert Winthrop asked, raising her lorgnette.

She mumbled through the blurred carbon sheet. Yes; it was a scene from a play.

'About a false Duke; and a Princess disguised as a boy; then the long lost heir turns out to be the beggar, because of a mole on his cheek; and Carinthia—that's the Duke's daughter, only she's been lost in a cave— falls in love with Ferdinando who had been put into a basket as a baby by an aged crone. And they marry. That's I think what happens,' she said, looking up from the programme.

'*Play out the play*,' great Eliza commanded. An aged crone tottered forward.

('Mrs Otter of the End House,' someone murmured.)

She sat herself on a packing case, and made motions, plucking her dishevelled locks and rocking herself from side to side as if she were an aged beldame in a chimney corner.

('The crone, who saved the rightful heir,' Mrs Winthrop explained.)

[80]

'Twas a winter's night (she croaked out)
*I mind me that, I to whom all's one now, summer or
    winter.*
You say the sun shines? I believe you, Sir.
'Oh but it's winter, and the fog's abroad'
All's one to Elsbeth, summer or winter,
By the fireside, in the chimney corner, telling her beads.
I've cause to tell 'em.
Each bead (she held a bead between thumb and finger)
A crime!
'Twas a winter's night, before cockcrow,
Yet the cock did crow ere he left me—
The man with a hood on his face, and the bloody hands
And the babe in the basket.
'Tee hee' he mewed, as who should say 'I want my toy'
Poor witling!
'Tee hee, tee hee!' I could not slay him!
For that, Mary in Heaven forgive me
The sins I've sinned before cockcrow!
Down to the creek i' the dawn I slipped
Where the gull haunts and the heron stands
Like a stake on the edge of the marshes . . .
Who's here?
(Three young men swaggered on to the stage and
    accosted her)
—'Are you come to torture me, Sirs?
There is little blood in this arm,
(she extended her skinny forearm from her ragged shift)
Saints in Heaven preserve me!'

She bawled. They bawled. All together they
bawled, and so loud that it was difficult to make out

what they were saying: apparently it was: *Did she remember concealing a child in a cradle among the rushes some twenty years previously? A babe in a basket, crone! A babe in a basket?* they bawled. *The wind howls and the bittern shrieks*, she replied.

'There is little blood in my arm,' Isabella repeated.

That was all she heard. There was such a medley of things going on, what with the beldame's deafness, the bawling of the youths, and the confusion of the plot that she could make nothing of it.

Did the plot matter? She shifted and looked over her right shoulder. The plot was only there to beget emotion. There were only two emotions: love; and hate. There was no need to puzzle out the plot. Perhaps Miss La Trobe meant that when she cut this knot in the centre?

Don't bother about the plot: the plot's nothing.

But what was happening? The Prince had come.

Plucking up his sleeve, the beldame recognized the mole; and, staggering back in her chair, shrieked:

My child! My child!

Recognition followed. The young Prince (Albert Perry) was almost smothered in the withered arms of the beldame. Then suddenly he started apart.

'*Look where she comes!*' he cried.

They all looked where she came—Sylvia Edwards in white satin.

Who came? Isa looked. The nightingale's song? The pearl in night's black ear? Love embodied.

[82]

All arms were raised; all faces stared.

'*Hail, sweet Carinthia!*' said the Prince, sweeping his hat off. And she to him, raising her eyes:

'*My love! My lord!*'

'It was enough. Enough. Enough,' Isa repeated.

All else was verbiage, repetition.

The beldame meanwhile, because that was enough, had sunk back on her chair, the beads dangling from her fingers.

'*Look to the beldame there—old Elsbeth's sick!*'
(They crowded round her)
Dead, Sirs!

She fell back lifeless. The crowd drew away. Peace, let her pass. She to whom all's one now, summer or winter.

Peace was the third emotion. Love. Hate. Peace. Three emotions made the ply of human life. Now the priest, whose cotton wool moustache confused his utterance, stepped forward and pronounced benediction.

From the distaff of life's tangled skein, unloose her hands
(They unloosed her hands)
Of her frailty, let nothing now remembered be.
*Call for the robin redbreast and the wren.**
And roses fall your crimson pall.
(Petals were strewn from wicker baskets)
Cover the corpse. Sleep well.
(They covered the corpse)
On you, fair Sirs (he turned to the happy couple)

[83]

Let Heaven rain benediction!
Haste ere the envying sun
Night's curtain hath undone. Let music sound
And the free air of Heaven waft you to your slumber!
Lead on the dance!

The gramophone blared. Dukes, priests, shepherds, pilgrims and serving men took hands and danced. The idiot scampered in and out. Hands joined, heads knocking, they danced round the majestic figure of the Elizabethan age personified by Mrs Clark, licensed to sell tobacco, on her soap box.

It was a mellay; a medley; an entrancing spectacle (to William) of dappled light and shade on half clothed, fantastically coloured, leaping, jerking, swinging legs and arms. He clapped till his palms stung.

Mrs Manresa applauded loudly. Somehow she was the Queen; and he (Giles) was the surly hero.

'Bravo! Bravo!' she cried, and her enthusiasm made the surly hero squirm on his seat. Then the great lady in the bath chair, the lady whose marriage with the local peer had obliterated in his trashy title a name that had been a name when there were brambles and briars where the Church now stood—so indigenous was she that even her body, crippled by arthritis, resembled an uncouth, nocturnal animal, now nearly extinct—clapped and laughed loud—the sudden laughter of a startled jay.

'Ha, ha, ha!' she laughed and clutched the arms of her chair with ungloved twisted hands.

A-maying, a-maying, they bawled. *In and out and round about, a-maying, a-maying . . .*

It didn't matter what the words were; or who sang what. Round and round they whirled, intoxicated by the music. Then, at a sign from Miss La Trobe behind the tree, the dance stopped. A procession formed. Great Eliza descended from her soap box. Taking her skirts in her hand, striding with long strides, surrounded by Dukes and Princes, followed by the lovers arm in arm, with Albert the idiot playing in and out, and the corpse on its bier concluding the procession, the Elizabethan age passed from the scene.

'Curse! Blast! Damn 'em!' Miss La Trobe in her rage stubbed her toe against a root. Here was her downfall; here was the Interval. Writing this skimble-skamble stuff* in her cottage, she had agreed to cut the play here; a slave to her audience,—to Mrs Sands's grumble—about tea; about dinner;—she had gashed the scene here. Just as she had brewed emotion, she spilt it. So she signalled: Phyllis! And, summoned, Phyllis popped up on the mat again in the middle.

Gentles and simples, I address you all (she piped.)
Our act is done, our scene is over.
Past is the day of crone and lover.
The bud has flowered; the flower has fallen.
But soon will rise another dawning,
For time whose children small we be

[85]

Hath in his keeping, you shall see,
You shall see . . .

Her voice petered out. No one was listening. Heads
bent, they read 'Interval' on the programme. And,
cutting short her words, the megaphone announced
in plain English: 'An interval'. Half an hour's interval,
for tea. Then the gramophone blared out:

> *Armed against fate,*
> *The valiant Rhoderick,*
> *Bold and blatant,*
> *Firm, elatant, etc., etc.*

At that, the audience stirred. Some rose briskly;
others stooped, retrieving walking-sticks, hats, bags.
And then, as they raised themselves and turned about,
the music modulated. The music chanted: *Dispersed
are we*. It moaned: *Dispersed are we*. It lamented:
Dispersed are we, as they streamed, spotting the grass
with colour, across the lawns, and down the paths:
Dispersed are we.

Mrs Manresa took up the strain. *Dispersed are we.*
'Freely, boldly, fearing no one' (she pushed a deck-
chair out of her way). 'Youths and maidens' (she
glanced behind her; but Giles had his back turned).
'Follow, follow, follow me . . . Oh Mr Parker, what
a pleasure to see *you* here! I'm for tea!'

'Dispersed are we,' Isabella followed her, humming. 'All is over. The wave has broken. Left us stranded, high and dry. Single, separate on the shingle. Broken is the three-fold ply . . . Now I follow' (she pushed her chair back . . . The man in grey was lost in the crowd by the ilex) 'that old strumpet' (she invoked Mrs Manresa's tight, flowered figure in front of her) 'to have tea.'

Dodge remained behind. 'Shall I', he murmured, 'go or stay? Slip out some other way? Or follow, follow, follow the dispersing company?'

Dispersed are we, the music wailed; *dispersed are we*. Giles remained like a stake in the tide of the flowing company.

'Follow?' He kicked his chair back. 'Whom? Where?' He stubbed his light tennis shoes on the wood. 'Nowhere. Anywhere.' Stark still he stood.

Here Cobbet of Cobbs Corner, alone under the monkey puzzle tree, rose and muttered: 'What was in her mind, eh? What idea lay behind, eh? What made her indue the antique with this glamour—this sham lure, and set 'em climbing, climbing, climbing up the monkey puzzle tree?'

Dispersed are we, the music wailed. *Dispersed are we*. He turned and sauntered slowly after the retreating company.

Now Lucy, retrieving her bag from beneath the seat, chirruped to her brother:

'Bart, my dear, come with me . . . D'you remember,

when we were children, the play we acted in the nursery?'

He remembered. Red Indians the game was; a reed with a note wrapped up in a pebble.

'But for us, my old Cindy'—he picked up his hat—'the game's over.' The glare and the stare and the beat of the tom-tom, he meant. He gave her his arm. Off they strolled. And Mr Page, the reporter, noted, 'Mrs Swithin: Mr B. Oliver,' then turning, added further 'Lady Haslip, of Haslip Manor', as he spied that old lady wheeled in her chair by her footman winding up the procession.

To the valediction of the gramophone hid in the bushes the audience departed. *Dispersed*, it wailed, *Dispersed are we*.

Now Miss La Trobe stepped from her hiding. Flowing, and streaming, on the grass, on the gravel, still for one moment she held them together—the dispersing company. Hadn't she, for twenty-five minutes, made them see? A vision imparted was relief from agony ... for one moment ... one moment. Then the music petered out on the last word *we*. She heard the breeze rustle in the branches. She saw Giles Oliver with his back to the audience. Also Cobbet of Cobbs Corner. She hadn't made them see. It was a failure, another damned failure! As usual. Her vision escaped her. And turning, she strode to the actors, undressing, down in the hollow, where butterflies feasted upon swords of silver paper; where the dish cloths in the shadow made pools of yellow.

Cobbet had out his watch. Three hours till seven, he noted; then water the plants. He turned.

Giles, nicking his chair into its notch, turned too, in the other direction. He took the short cut by the fields to the Barn. This dry summer the path was hard as brick across the fields. This dry summer the path was strewn with stones. He kicked—a flinty yellow stone, a sharp stone, edged as if cut by a savage for an arrow. A barbaric stone; a pre-historic. Stone-kicking was a child's game. He remembered the rules. By the rules of the game, one stone, the same stone, must be kicked to the goal. Say a gate, or a tree. He played it alone. The gate was a goal; to be reached in ten. The first kick was Manresa (lust). The second, Dodge (perversion). The third himself (coward). And the fourth and the fifth and all the others were the same.

He reached it in ten. There, couched in the grass, curled in an olive green ring, was a snake. Dead? No, choked with a toad in its mouth. The snake was unable to swallow; the toad was unable to die. A spasm made the ribs contract; blood oozed. It was birth the wrong way round—a monstrous inversion. So, raising his foot, he stamped on them. The mass crushed and slithered. The white canvas on his tennis shoes was bloodstained and sticky. But it was action. Action relieved him. He strode to the Barn, with blood on his shoes.

[89]

The Barn, the Noble Barn, the barn that had been built over seven hundred years ago and reminded some people of a Greek temple, others of the middle ages, most people of an age before their own, scarcely anybody of the present moment, was empty.

The great doors stood open. A shaft of light like a yellow banner sloped from roof to floor. Festoons of paper roses, left over from the Coronation, drooped from the rafters. A long table, on which stood an urn, plates and cups, cakes and bread and butter, stretched across one end. The Barn was empty. Mice slid in and out of holes or stood upright, nibbling. Swallows were busy with straw in pockets of earth in the rafters. Countless beetles and insects of various sorts burrowed in the dry wood. A stray bitch had made the dark corner where the sacks stood a lying-in ground for her puppies. All these eyes, expanding and narrowing, some adapted to light, others to darkness, looked from different angles and edges. Minute nibblings and rustlings broke the silence. Whiffs of sweetness and richness veined the air. A bluebottle had settled on the cake and stabbed its yellow rock with its short drill. A butterfly sunned itself sensuously on a sunlit yellow plate.

But Mrs Sands was approaching. She was pushing her way through the crowd. She had turned the corner. She could see the great open door. But butterflies she never saw; mice were only black pellets in kitchen drawers; moths she bundled in her hands

[90]

and put out of the window. Bitches suggested only
servant girls misbehaving. Had there been a cat she
would have seen it—any cat, a starved cat with a
patch of mange on its rump opened the flood gates of
her childless heart. But there was no cat. The Barn
was empty. And so running, panting, set upon reaching the Barn and taking up her station behind the tea
urn before the company came, she reached the Barn.
And the butterfly rose and the bluebottle.

Following her in a scud came the servants and
helpers—David, John, Irene, Lois. Water boiled.
Steam issued. Cake was sliced. Swallows swooped
from rafter to rafter. And the company entered.

'This fine old Barn . . .' said Mrs Manresa, stopping
in the doorway. It was not for her to press ahead of
the villagers. It was for her, moved by the beauty of
the Barn, to stand still; to draw aside; to gaze; to let
other people come first.

'We have one, much like it, at Lathom,' said Mrs
Parker, stopping, for the same reasons. 'Perhaps,' she
added, 'not quite so large.'

The villagers hung back. Then, hesitating, dribbled
past.

'And the decorations . . .' said Mrs Manresa, looking round for someone to congratulate. She stood
smiling, waiting. Then old Mrs Swithin came in. She
was gazing up too, but not at the decorations. At the
swallows apparently.

'They come every year,' she said, 'the same birds.'

Mrs Manresa smiled benevolently, humouring the old lady's whimsy. It was unlikely, she thought, that the birds were the same.

'The decorations, I suppose, are left over from the Coronation,' said Mrs Parker. 'We kept ours too. We built a village hall.'

Mrs Manresa laughed. She remembered. An anecdote was on the tip of her tongue, about a public lavatory built to celebrate the same occasion, and how the Mayor . . . Could she tell it? No. The old lady, gazing at the swallows, looked too refined. 'Refeened'—Mrs Manresa qualified the word to her own advantage, thus confirming her approval of the wild child she was, whose nature was somehow 'just human nature'. Somehow she could span the old lady's 'refeenment', also the boy's fun—Where was that nice fellow Giles? She couldn't see him; nor Bill either. The villagers still hung back. They must have someone to start the ball rolling.

'Well, I'm dying for my tea!' she said in her public voice; and strode forward. She laid hold of a thick china mug. Mrs Sands giving precedence, of course, to one of the gentry, filled it at once. David gave her cake. She was the first to drink, the first to bite. The villagers still hung back. 'It's all my eye about democracy,' she concluded. So did Mrs Parker, taking her mug too. The people looked to them. They led; the rest followed.

'What delicious tea!' each exclaimed, disgusting

though it was, like rust boiled in water, and the cake fly-blown. But they had a duty to society.

'They come every year,' said Mrs Swithin, ignoring the fact that she spoke to the empty air. 'From Africa.' As they had come, she supposed, when the Barn was a swamp.

The Barn filled. Fumes rose. China clattered; voices chattered. Isa pressed her way to the table.

'Dispersed are we,' she murmured. And held her cup out to be filled. She took it. 'Let me turn away', she murmured, turning, 'from the array'—she looked desolately round her—'of china faces, glazed and hard. Down the ride, that leads under the nut tree and the may tree, away, till I come to the wishing well, where the washerwoman's little boy—' she dropped sugar, two lumps, into her tea, 'dropped a pin. He got his horse, so they say. But what wish should I drop into the well?' She looked around. She could not see the man in grey, the gentleman farmer; nor anyone known to her. 'That the waters should cover me', she added, 'of the wishing well.'

The noise of china and chatter drowned her murmur. 'Sugar for you?' they were saying. 'Just a spot of milk? And you?' 'Tea without milk or sugar. That's the way I like it.' 'A bit too strong? Let me add water.'

'That's what I wished,' Isa added, 'when I dropped my pin. Water. Water . . .'

'I must say,' the voice said behind her, 'it's brave

of the King and Queen.* They're said to be going to India. She looks such a dear. Someone I know said his hair . . .'

'There,' Isa mused, 'would the dead leaf fall, when the leaves fall, on the water. Should I mind not again to see may tree or nut tree? Not again to hear on the trembling spray the thrush sing, or to see, dipping and diving as if he skimmed waves in the air, the yellow woodpecker?'

She was looking at the canary yellow festoons left over from the Coronation.

'I thought they said Canada, not India,' the voice said behind her back. To which the other voice answered: 'D'you believe what the papers say? For instance, about the Duke of Windsor.* He landed on the south coast. Queen Mary met him. She'd been buying furniture—that's a fact. And the papers say she met him . . .'

'Alone, under a tree, the withered tree that keeps all day murmuring of the sea, and hears the Rider gallop . . .'

Isa filled in the phrase. Then she started. William Dodge was by her side.

He smiled. She smiled. They were conspirators; each murmuring some song my uncle taught me.

'It's the play,' she said. 'The play keeps running in my head.'

'Hail, sweet Carinthia. My love. My life,' he quoted.

'My lord, my liege,' she bowed ironically.

She was handsome. He wanted to see her, not against the tea urn, but with her glass green eyes and thick body, the neck was broad as a pillar, against an arum lily or a vine. He wished she would say: 'Come along. I'll show you the greenhouse, the pig sty, or the stable.' But she said nothing, and they stood there holding their cups, remembering the play. Then he saw her face change, as if she had got out of one dress and put on another. A small boy battled his way through the crowd, striking against skirts and trousers as if he were swimming blindly.

'Here!' she cried raising her arm.

He made a bee-line for her. He was her little boy, apparently, her son, her George. She gave him cake; then a mug of milk. Then Nurse came up. Then again she changed her dress. This time, from the expression in her eyes it was apparently something in the nature of a strait waistcoat. Hirsute, handsome, virile, the young man in blue jacket and brass buttons, standing in a beam of dusty light, was her husband. And she his wife. Their relations, as he had noted at lunch, were as people say in novels 'strained'. As he had noted at the play, her bare arm had raised itself nervously to her shoulder when she turned—looking for whom? But here he was; and the muscular, the hirsute, the virile plunged him into emotions in which the mind had no share. He forgot how she would have looked against vine leaf in a greenhouse. Only at

Giles he looked; and looked and looked. Of whom was he thinking as he stood with his face turned? Not of Isa. Of Mrs Manresa?

Mrs Manresa half-way down the Barn had gulped her cup of tea. How can I rid myself, she asked, of Mrs Parker? If they were of her own class, how they bored her—her own sex! Not the class below—cooks, shopkeepers, farmers' wives; nor the class above—peeresses, countesses; it was the women of her own class that bored her. So she left Mrs Parker, abruptly.

'Oh Mrs Moore,' she hailed the keeper's wife. 'What did you think of it? And what did baby think of it?' Here she pinched baby. 'I thought it every bit as good as anything I'd seen in London . . . But we mustn't be outdone. We'll have a play of our own. In *our* Barn. We'll show 'em' (here she winked obliquely at the table; so many bought cakes, so few made at home) 'how *we* do it.'

Then cracking her jokes, she turned; saw Giles; caught his eye; and swept him in, beckoning. He came. And what—she looked down—had he done with his shoes? They were bloodstained. Vaguely some sense that he had proved his valour for her admiration flattered her. If vague it was sweet. Taking him in tow, she felt: I am the Queen, he my hero, my sulky hero.

'That's Mrs Neale!' she exclaimed. 'A perfect marvel of a woman, aren't you, Mrs Neale! She runs our post office, Mrs Neale. She can do sums in her head, can't you, Mrs Neale? Twenty-five halfpenny stamps, two packets of stamped envelopes and a packet of postcards—how much does that come to, Mrs Neale?'

Mrs Neale laughed; Mrs Manresa laughed; Giles too smiled, and looked down at his shoes.

She drew him down the Barn, in and out, from one to another. She knew 'em all. Every one was a thorough good sort. No, she wouldn't allow it, not for a moment—Pinsent's bad leg. 'No, no. We're not going to take that for an excuse, Pinsent.' If he couldn't bowl, he could bat. Giles agreed. A fish on a line meant the same to him and Pinsent; also jays and magpies. Pinsent stayed on the land; Giles went to an office. That was all. And she was a thorough good sort, making him feel less of an audience, more of an actor, going round the Barn in her wake.

Then, at the end by the door, they came upon the old couple, Lucy and Bartholomew, sitting on their Windsor chairs.

Chairs had been reserved for them. Mrs Sands had sent them tea. It would have caused more bother than it was worth—asserting the democratic principle; standing in the crowd at the table.

'Swallows,' said Lucy, holding her cup, looking at the birds. Excited by the company they were flitting from rafter to rafter. Across Africa, across France they had come to nest here. Year after year they came. Before there was a channel, when the earth, upon which the Windsor chair* was planted, was a riot of rhododendrons, and humming birds quivered at the mouths of scarlet trumpets, as she had read that morning in her Outline of History, they had come . . . Here Bart rose from his chair.

But Mrs Manresa absolutely refused to take his seat. 'Go on sitting, go on sitting,' she pressed him down again. 'I'll squat on the floor.' She squatted. The surly knight remained in attendance.

'And what did you think of the play?' she asked.

Bartholomew looked at his son. His son remained silent.

'And you Mrs Swithin?' Mrs Manresa pressed the old lady.

Lucy mumbled, looking at the swallows.

'I was hoping you'd tell me,' said Mrs Manresa. 'Was it an old play? Was it a new play?'

No one answered.

'Look!' Lucy exclaimed.

'The birds?' said Mrs Manresa, looking up.

There was a bird with a straw in its beak; and the straw dropped.

Lucy clapped her hands. Giles turned away. She was mocking him as usual, laughing.

'Going?' said Bartholomew. 'Time for the next act?'

And he heaved himself up from his chair. Regardless of Mrs Manresa and of Lucy, off he strolled too.

'Swallow, my sister, O sister swallow,' he muttered, feeling for his cigar case, following his son.

Mrs Manresa was nettled. What for had she squatted on the floor then? Were her charms fading? Both were gone. But, woman of action as she was, deserted by the male sex, she was not going to suffer tortures of boredom from the refeened old lady. Up she scrambled, putting her hands to hair as if it were high time that she went too, though it was nothing of the kind and her hair was perfectly tidy. Cobbet in his corner saw through her little game. He had known human nature in the East. It was the same in the West. Plants remained—the carnation, the zinnia, and the geranium. Automatically he consulted his watch; noted time to water at seven; and observed the little game of the woman following the man to the table in the West as in the East.

William at the table, now attached to Mrs Parker and Isa, watched him approach. Armed and valiant, bold and blatant, firm elatant—the popular march tune rang in his head. And the fingers of William's left hand closed firmly, surreptitiously, as the hero approached.

Mrs Parker was deploring to Isa in a low voice the village idiot.

'Oh that idiot!' she was saying. But Isa was immobile, watching her husband. She could feel the

Manresa in his wake. She could hear in the dusk in their bedroom the usual explanation. It made no difference; his infidelity—but hers did.

'The idiot?' William answered Mrs Parker for her. 'He's in the tradition.'

'But surely,' said Mrs Parker, and told Giles how creepy the idiot—'We have one in our village'—had made her feel. 'Surely, Mr Oliver, we're more civilized?'

'*We?*' said Giles. '*We?*' He looked, once, at William. He knew not his name; but what his left hand was doing. It was a bit of luck—that he could despise him, not himself. Also Mrs Parker. But not Isa—not his wife. She had not spoken to him, not one word. Nor looked at him either.

'Surely,' said Mrs Parker, looking from one to the other. 'Surely we are?'

Giles then did what to Isa was his little trick; shut his lips; frowned; and took up the pose of one who bears the burden of the world's woe, making money for her to spend.

'No,' said Isa, as plainly as words could say it. 'I don't admire you,' and looked, not at his face, but at his feet. 'Silly little boy, with blood on his boots.'

Giles shifted his feet. Whom then did she admire? Not Dodge. That he could take for certain. Who else? Some man he knew. Some man, he was sure, in the Barn. Which man? He looked round him.

Then Mr Streatfield, the clergyman, interrupted. He was carrying cups.

'So I shake hands with my heart!' he exclaimed, nodding his handsome, grizzled head and depositing his burden safely.

Mrs Parker took the tribute to herself.

'Mr Streatfield!' she exclaimed. 'Doing all the work! While we stand gossiping!'

'Like to see the greenhouse?' said Isa suddenly, turning to William Dodge.

O not now, he could have cried. But had to follow, leaving Giles to welcome the approaching Manresa, who had him in thrall.

The path was narrow. Isa went ahead. And she was broad; she fairly filled the path, swaying slightly as she walked, and plucking a leaf here and there from the hedge.

'Fly then, follow,' she hummed, 'the dappled herds in the cedar grove, who, sporting, play, the red with the roe, the stag with the doe. Fly, away. I grieving stay. Alone I linger, I pluck the bitter herb by the ruined wall, the churchyard wall, and press its sour, its sweet, its sour, long grey leaf, so, twixt thumb and finger . . .'

She threw away the shred of Old Man's Beard that she had picked in passing and kicked open the greenhouse door. Dodge had lagged behind. She waited.

She picked up a knife from the plank. He saw her standing against the green glass, the fig tree, and the blue hydrangea, knife in hand.

'She spake,' Isa murmured. 'And from her bosom's snowy antre drew the gleaming blade. "Plunge blade!" she said. And struck. "Faithless!" she cried. Knife, too! It broke. So too my heart,' she said.

She was smiling ironically as he came up.

'I wish the play didn't run in my head,' she said. Then she sat down on a plank under the vine. And he sat beside her. The little grapes above them were green buds; the leaves thin and yellow as the web between birds' claws.

'Still the play?' he asked. She nodded. 'That was your son,' he said, 'in the Barn?'

She had a daughter too, she told him, in the cradle.

'And you—married?' she asked. From her tone he knew she guessed, as women always guessed, everything. They knew at once they had nothing to fear, nothing to hope. At first they resented—serving as statues in a greenhouse. Then they liked it. For then they could say—as she did—whatever came into their heads. And hand him, as she handed him, a flower.

'There's something for your buttonhole, Mr . . .' she said, handing him a sprig of scented geranium.

'I'm William,' he said, taking the furry leaf and pressing it between thumb and finger.

'I'm Isa,' she answered. Then they talked as if they

had known each other all their lives; which was odd, she said, as they always did, considering she'd known him perhaps one hour. Weren't they, though, conspirators, seekers after hidden faces? That confessed, she paused and wondered, as they always did, why they could speak so plainly to each other. And added: 'Perhaps because we've never met before, and never shall again.'

'The doom of sudden death hanging over us,' he said. 'There's no retreating and advancing'—he was thinking of the old lady showing him the house—'for us as for them.'

The future shadowed their present, like the sun coming through the many-veined transparent vine leaf; a criss-cross of lines making no pattern.

They had left the greenhouse door open, and now music came through it. A.B.C., A.B.C., A.B.C.— someone was practising scales. C.A.T. C.A.T. C.A.T. . . . Then the separate letters made one word 'Cat'. Other words followed. It was a simple tune, like a nursery rhyme—

> The King is in his counting house,
> Counting out his money,
> The Queen is in her parlour
> Eating bread and honey

They listened. Another voice, a third voice, was saying something simple. And they sat on in the greenhouse, on the plank with the vine over them, listening to Miss La Trobe or whoever it was, practising her scales.

He could not find his son. He had lost him in the crowd. So old Bartholomew left the Barn, and went to his own room, holding his cheroot and murmuring:

'O sister swallow, O sister swallow,
How can thy heart be full of the spring?'*

'How can my heart be full of the spring?' he said aloud, standing in front of the book case. Books: the treasured life-blood of immortal spirits. Poets; the legislators of mankind. Doubtless, it was so. But Giles was unhappy. 'How can my heart, how can my heart,' he repeated, puffing at his cheroot. 'Condemned in life's infernal mine, condemned in solitude to pine . . .'* Arms akimbo, he stood in front of his country gentleman's library. Garibaldi; Wellington;* Irrigation Officers' Reports; and Hibbert on the Diseases of the Horse. A great harvest the mind had reaped; but for all this, compared with his son, he did not care one damn.

'What's the use, what's the use,' he sank down into his chair muttering. 'O sister swallow, O sister swallow, of singing your song?' The dog, who had followed him, flopped down on to the floor at his feet. Flanks sucked in and out, the long nose resting on his paws, a fleck of foam on the nostril, there he was, his familiar spirit, his Afghan hound.

The door trembled and stood half open. That was Lucy's way of coming in—as if she did not know what she would find. Really! It was her brother! And his dog! She seemed to see them for the first time. Was it that she had no body? Up in the clouds, like an air ball, her mind touched ground now and then with a shock of surprise. There was nothing in her to weight a man like Giles to the earth.

She perched on the edge of a chair like a bird on a telegraph wire before starting for Africa.

'Swallow, my sister, O sister swallow ...' he murmured.

From the garden—the window was open—came the sound of someone practising scales. A.B.C. A.B.C. A.B.C. Then the separate letters formed one word 'Dog'. Then a phrase. It was a simple tune, another voice speaking.

> 'Hark hark, the dogs do bark
> The beggars are coming to town ...'*

Then it languished and lengthened, and became a waltz. As they listened and looked—out into the garden—the trees tossing and the birds swirling seemed called out of their private lives, out of their separate avocations, and made to take part.

The lamp of love burns high, over the dark cedar groves,
The lamp of love shines clear, clear as a star in the sky ...

Old Bartholomew tapped his fingers on his knee in time to the tune.

Leave your casement and come, lady, I love till I die,

He looked sardonically at Lucy, perched on her chair. How, he wondered, had she ever borne children?

For all are dancing, retreating and advancing,
The moth and the dragon fly . . .

She was thinking, he supposed, God is peace. God is love. For she belonged to the unifiers; he to the separatists.

Then the tune with its feet always on the same spot, became sugared, insipid; bored a hole with its perpetual invocation to perpetual adoration. Had it—he was ignorant of musical terms—gone into the minor key?

For this day and this dance and this merry, merry May
Will be over (he tapped his forefinger on his knee)
With the cutting of the clover this retreating and advanc-
    ing—the swifts seemed to have shot beyond their
    orbits—
Will be over, over, over,
And the ice will dart its splinter, and the winter,
O the winter, will fill the grate with ashes,
And there'll be no glow, no glow on the log.

He knocked the ash off his cheroot and rose.

'So we must,' said Lucy; as if he had said aloud, 'It's time to go.'

*

The audience was assembling. The music was sum-
moning them. Down the paths, across the lawns they
were streaming again. There was Mrs Manresa, with
Giles at her side, heading the procession. In taut
plump curves her scarf blew round her shoulders.
The breeze was rising. She looked, as she crossed the
lawn to the strains of the gramophone, goddess-like,
buoyant, abundant, her cornucopia running over.
Bartholomew, following, blessed the power of the
human body to make the earth fruitful. Giles would
keep his orbit so long as she weighted him to the
earth. She stirred the stagnant pool of his old heart
even—where bones lay buried, but the dragon flies
shot and the grass trembled as Mrs Manresa advanced
across the lawn to the strains of the gramophone.

Feet crunched the gravel. Voices chattered. The
inner voice, the other voice was saying: How can we
deny that this brave music, wafted from the bushes,
is expressive of some inner harmony? 'When we
wake' (some were thinking) 'the day breaks us with
its hard mallet blows.' 'The office' (some were thinking) 'compels disparity. Scattered, shattered, hither
thither summoned by the bell. "Ping-ping-ping"
that's the phone. "Forward!" "Serving!"—that's the
shop.' So we answer to the infernal, agelong and
eternal order issued from on high. And obey. 'Working, serving, pushing, striving, earning wages—to be
spent—here? Oh dear no. Now? No, by and by.
When ears are deaf and the heart is dry.'

Here Cobbet of Cobbs Corner who had stooped—
there was a flower—was pressed on by people pushing from behind.

For I hear music, they were saying. Music wakes
us. Music makes us see the hidden, join the broken.
Look and listen. See the flowers, how they ray their
redness, whiteness, silverness and blue. And the trees
with their many-tongued much syllabling, their green
and yellow leaves hustle us and shuffle us, and bid us,
like the starlings, and the rooks, come together,
crowd together, to chatter and make merry while the
red cow moves forward and the black cow stands
still.

The audience had reached their seats. Some sat
down; others stood a moment, turned, and looked at
the view. The stage was empty; the actors were still
dressing up among the bushes. The audience turned
to one another and began to talk. Scraps and fragments reached Miss La Trobe where she stood, script
in hand, behind the tree.

'They're not ready . . . I hear 'em laughing' (they
were saying). '. . . Dressing up. That's the great thing,
dressing up. And it's pleasant now, the sun's not so
hot . . . That's one good the war brought us—longer
days . . . Where did we leave off? D'you remember?
The Elizabethans . . . Perhaps she'll reach the present,
if she skips . . . D'you think people change? Their
clothes, of course . . . But I meant ourselves . . .

Clearing out a cupboard, I found my father's old top hat . . . But ourselves—do we change?'

'No, I don't go by politicians. I've a friend who's been to Russia. He says . . . And my daughter, just back from Rome, she says the common people, in the cafés, hate Dictators . . . Well, different people say different things . . .'

'Did you see it in the papers—the case about the dog? D'you believe dogs can't have puppies? . . . And Queen Mary and the Duke of Windsor on the south coast? . . . D'you believe what's in the papers? I ask the butcher or the grocer . . . That's Mr Streatfield, carrying a hurdle . . . The good clergyman, I say, does more work for less pay than all the lot . . . It's the wives that make the trouble . . .'

'And what about the Jews? The refugees . . . the Jews . . . People like ourselves, beginning life again . . . But it's always been the same . . . My old mother, who's over eighty, can remember . . . Yes, she still reads without glasses . . . How amazing! Well, don't they say, after eighty . . . Now they're coming . . . No, that's nothing . . . I'd make it penal, leaving litter. But then, who's, my husband says, to collect the fines? . . . Ah there she is, Miss La Trobe, over there, behind that tree . . .'

Over there behind the tree Miss La Trobe gnashed her teeth. She crushed her manuscript. The actors delayed. Every moment the audience slipped the noose; split up into scraps and fragments.

'Music!' she signalled. 'Music!'

'What's the origin', said a voice, 'of the expression "with a flea in his ear"?'

Down came her hand peremptorily. 'Music, music,' she signalled.

And the gramophone began A.B.C., A.B.C.

> *The King is in his counting house*
> *Counting out his money,*
> *The Queen is in her parlour*
> *Eating bread and honey . . .*

Miss La Trobe watched them sink down peacefully into the nursery rhyme. She watched them fold their hands and compose their faces. Then she beckoned. And at last, with a final touch to her head dress, which had been giving trouble, Mabel Hopkins strode from the bushes, and took her place on the raised ground facing the audience.

Eyes fed on her as fish rise to a crumb of bread on the water. Who was she? What did she represent? She was beautiful—very. Her cheeks had been powdered; her colour glowed smooth and clear underneath. Her grey satin robe (a bedspread), pinned in stone-like folds, gave her the majesty of a statue. She carried a sceptre and a little round orb. England was she? Queen Anne was she? Who was she? She spoke too low at first; all they heard was

. . . reason holds sway.

Old Bartholomew applauded.

'Hear! Hear!' he cried. 'Bravo! Bravo!'

Thus encouraged Reason spoke out.

Time, leaning on his sickle, stands amazed. While commerce from her Cornucopia pours the mingled tribute of her different ores. In distant mines the savage sweats; and from the reluctant earth the painted pot is shaped. At my behest, the armed warrior lays his shield aside; the heathen leaves the Altar steaming with unholy sacrifice. The violet and the eglantine over the riven earth their flowers entwine. No longer fears the unwary wanderer the poisoned snake. And in the helmet, yellow bees their honey make.

She paused. A long line of villagers in sacking were passing in and out of the trees behind her.

Digging and delving, ploughing and sowing they were singing, but the wind blew their words away.

Beneath the shelter of my flowing robe (she resumed, extending her arms) *the arts arise. Music for me unfolds her heavenly harmony. At my behest the miser leaves his hoard untouched; at peace the mother sees her children play . . . Her children play . . .* she repeated, and, waving her sceptre, figures advanced from the bushes.

Let swains and nymphs lead on the play, while Zephyr sleeps, and the unruly tribes of Heaven confess my sway.

A merry little old tune was played on the

gramophone. Old Bartholomew joined his finger tips;
Mrs Manresa smoothed her skirts about her knees.

> *Young Damon said to Cynthia*
> *Come out now with the dawn*
> *And don your azure tippet*
> *And cast your cares adown*
> *For peace has come to England,*
> *And reason now holds sway.*
> *What pleasure lies in dreaming*
> *When blue and green's the day?*
> *Now cast your cares behind you.*
> *Night passes: here is Day.*

Digging and delving, the villagers sang passing in
single file in and out between the trees, *for the earth
is always the same, summer and winter and spring;
and spring and winter again; ploughing and sowing,
eating and growing; time passes . . .*

The wind blew the words away.

The dance stopped. The nymphs and swains withdrew. Reason held the centre of the stage alone. Her
arms extended, her robes flowing, holding orb and
sceptre, Mabel Hopkins stood sublimely looking over
the heads of the audience. The audience gazed at her.
She ignored the audience. Then while she gazed,
helpers from the bushes arranged round her what
appeared to be the three sides of a room. In the
middle they stood a table. On the table they placed a
china tea service. Reason surveyed this domestic

scene from her lofty eminence unmoved. There was a
pause.

'Another scene from another play, I suppose,' said
Mrs Elmhurst, referring to her programme. She read
out for the benefit of her husband, who was deaf:
'*Where there's a Will there's a Way*. That's the name
of the play. And the characters ...' She read out:
'Lady Harpy Harraden, in love with Sir Spaniel
Lilyliver. Deb, her maid. Flavinda, her niece, in love
with Valentine. Sir Spaniel Lilyliver, in love with
Flavinda. Sir Smirking Peace-be-with-you-all, a clergyman. Lord and Lady Fribble. Valentine, in love
with Flavinda. What names for real people! But
look—here they come!'

Out they came from the bushes—men in flowered
waistcoats, white waistcoats and buckled shoes;
women wearing brocades tucked up, hooped and
draped; glass stars, blue ribands and imitation pearls
made them look the very image of Lords and Ladies.

'The first scene', Mrs Elmhurst whispered into her
husband's ear, 'is Lady Harraden's dressing-room ...
That's her ...' She pointed. 'Mrs Otter, I think, from
the End House; but she's wonderfully made up. And
that's Deb her maid. Who she is, I don't know.'

'Hush, hush, hush,' someone protested.

Mrs Elmhurst dropped her programme. The play
had begun.

Lady Harpy Harraden entered her dressing-room,
followed by Deb her maid.

LADY H.H. . . . *Give me the pounce-box.** *Then the patch.** *Hand me the mirror, girl. So. Now my wig . . . A pox on the girl—she's dreaming!*

DEB . . . *I was thinking, my lady, what the gentleman said when he saw you in the Park.*

LADY H.H. (gazing in the glass) *So, so—what was it? Some silly trash! Cupid's dart—hah, hah! lighting his taper—tush—at my eyes . . . pooh! That was in milord's time, twenty years since . . . But now— what'll he say of me now?* (She looks in the mirror) *Sir Spaniel Lilyliver, I mean . . .* (a rap at the door) *Hark! That's his chaise at the door. Run child. Don't stand gaping.*

DEB . . . (going to the door) *Say? He'll rattle his tongue as a gambler rattles dice in a box. He'll find no words to fit you. He'll stand like a pig in a poke . . . Your servant, Sir Spaniel.*

Enter Sir Spaniel.

SIR S.L. . . . *Hail, my fair Saint! What, out o' bed so early? Methought, as I came along the Mall the air was something brighter than usual. Here's the reason . . . Venus, Aphrodite, upon my word a very galaxy, a constellation! As I'm a sinner, a very Aurora Borealis!*

(He sweeps his hat off.)

LADY H.H. *Oh flatterer, flatterer! I know your ways. But come. Sit down . . . A glass of Aqua Vitae.** *Take this seat, Sir Spaniel. I've something very private*

[114]

and particular to say to you . . . You had my letter, Sir?

Sir S.L. . . . *Pinned to my heart!*

(He strikes his breast.)

Lady H.H. . . . *I have a favour to ask of you, Sir.*

Sir S.L. . . . (singing) *What favour could fair Chloe ask that Damon would not get her? . . . O done with rhymes. Rhymes are still-a-bed. Let's speak prose. What can Asphodilla ask of her plain servant Lily-liver? Speak out, Madam. An ape with a ring in his nose, or a strong young jackanapes to tell tales of us when we're no longer here to tell truth about ourselves?*

Lady H.H. (flirting her fan) *Fie, fie, Sir Spaniel. You make me blush—you do indeed. But come closer.* (She shifts her seat nearer to him) *We don't want the whole world to hear us.*

Sir S.L. (aside) *Come closer? A pox on my life! The old hag stinks like a red herring that's been stood over head in a tar barrel!* (Aloud) *Your meaning, Madam? You were saying?*

Lady H.H. *I have a niece, Sir Spaniel, Flavinda by name.*

Sir S.L. (aside) *Why that's the girl I love, to be sure!* (Aloud) *You have a niece, Madam? I seem to remember hearing so. An only child, left by your brother, so I've heard, in your Ladyship's charge—him that perished at sea.*

[115]

LADY H.H. *The very same Sir. She's of age now and marriageable. I've kept her close as a weevil, Sir Spaniel, wrapped in the sere cloths of her virginity. Only maids about her, never a man to my knowledge, save Clout the serving man, who has a wart on his nose and a face like a nutgrater. Yet some fool has caught her fancy. Some gilded fly—some Harry, Dick; call him what you will.*

SIR S.L. (aside) *That's young Valentine, I warrant. I caught 'em at the play together.* (Aloud) *Say you so, Madam?*

LADY H.H. *She's not so ill favoured, Sir Spaniel— there's beauty in our line—but that a gentleman of taste and breeding like yourself now might take pity on her.*

SIR S.L. *Saving your presence, Madam. Eyes that have seen the sun are not so easily dazzled by the lesser lights—the Cassiopeias, Aldebarans, Great Bears and so on—A fig for them when the sun's up!*

LADY H.H. (ogling him) *You praise my hair-dresser, Sir, or my ear-rings* (she shakes her head).

SIR S.L. (aside) *She jingles like a she-ass at a fair! She's rigged like a barber's pole of a May Day.* (Aloud) *Your commands, Madam?*

LADY H.H. *Well Sir, t'was this way, Sir. Brother Bob, for my father was a plain country gentleman and would have none of the fancy names the foreigners brought with 'em—Asphodilla I call myself, but my Christian name's plain Sue—Brother Bob, as I was telling you, ran away to sea; and, so they say, became Emperor of the Indies; where the very stones are emeralds and the sheep-crop rubies. Which, for a tenderer-hearted man never lived, he would have brought back with him, Sir, to mend the family fortunes, Sir. But the brig, frigate or what they call it, for I've no head for sea terms, never crossed a ditch without saying the Lord's Prayer backwards, struck a rock. The Whale had him. But the cradle was by the bounty of Heaven washed ashore. With the girl in it; Flavinda here. What's more to the point, with the Will in it; safe and sound; wrapped in parchment. Brother Bob's Will. Deb there! Deb I say! Deb!*

(She hollas for Deb)

SIR S.L. (aside) *Ah hah! I smell a rat! A will, quotha! Where there's a Will there's a Way.*

LADY H.H. (bawling) *The Will, Deb! The Will! In the ebony box by the right hand of the escritoire opposite the window ... A pox on the girl! She's dreaming. It's these romances, Sir Spaniel—these romances. Can't see a candle gutter but it's her heart that's melting, or snuff a wick without reciting all the names in Cupid's Calendar ...*

(Enter Deb carrying a parchment)

LADY H.H. *So ... Give it here. The Will. Brother Bob's Will* (she mumbles over the Will).

LADY H.H. *To cut the matter short, Sir, for these*

[117]

lawyers even at the Antipodes are a long-winded race—

SIR S.L. *To match their ears, Ma'am—*

LADY H.H. *Very true, very true. To cut the matter short, Sir, my brother Bob left all he died possessed of to his only child Flavinda; with this proviso, mark ye. That she marry to her Aunt's liking. Her Aunt; that's me. Otherwise, mark ye, all—to wit ten bushels of diamonds; item of rubies; item two hundred square miles of fertile territory bounding the River Amazon to the Nor-Nor-East; item his snuff box; item his flageolet—he was always one to love a tune, Sir, Brother Bob; item six Macaws and as many Concubines as he had with him at the time of his decease—all this with other trifles needless to specify he left, mark ye, should she fail to marry to her Aunt's liking—that's me—to found a chapel, Sir Spaniel, where six poor Virgins should sing hymns in perpetuity for the repose of his soul—which, to speak the truth, Sir Spaniel, poor Brother Bob stands in need of, perambulating the Gulf Stream as he is and consorting with Syrens. But take it; read the Will yourself, Sir.*

SIR S.L. (reading) *'Must marry to her Aunt's liking.' That's plain enough.*

LADY H.H. *Her Aunt, Sir. That's me. That's plain enough.*

SIR S.L. (aside) *She speaks the truth there!* (Aloud) *You would have me understand, Madam . . .?*

LADY H.H. *Hist! Come closer. Let me whisper in*

*your ear . . . You and I have long entertained a high
opinion of one another, Sir Spaniel. Played at ball
together. Bound our wrists with daisy chains together.
If I mind aright, you called me little bride—'tis fifty
years since. We might have made a match of it, Sir
Spaniel, had fortune favoured . . . You take my meaning, Sir?*

Sir S.L. *Had it been written in letters of gold, fifty
feet high, visible from Paul's Churchyard to the Goat
and Compasses at Peckham,* it could have been no
plainer . . . Hist, I'll whisper it. I, Sir Spaniel Lilyliver,
do hereby bind myself to take thee—what's the name
of the green girl that was cast up in a lobster pot
covered with seaweed? Flavinda, eh? Flavinda, so—
to be my wedded wife—O for a lawyer to have it all
in writing!*

Lady H.H. *On condition, Sir Spaniel.*

Sir S.L. *On condition, Asphodilla.*

(Both speak together)

That the money is shared between us.

Lady H.H. *We want no lawyer to certify that!
Your hand on it, Sir Spaniel!*

Sir S.L. *Your lips Madam!*

(They embrace)

Sir S.L. *Pah! she stinks!*

*

'Ha! Ha! Ha!' laughed the indigenous old lady in her bathchair.

'Reason, begad! Reason!' exclaimed old Bartholomew, and looked at his son as if exhorting him to give over these womanish vapours and be a man, Sir.

Giles sat straight as a dart, his feet tucked under him.

Mrs Manresa had out her mirror and lipstick and attended to her lips and nose.

The gramophone, while the scene was removed, gently stated certain facts which everybody knows to be perfectly true. The tune said, more or less, how Eve, gathering her robes about her, stands reluctant still to let her dewy mantle fall. The herded flocks, the tune continued, in peace repose. The poor man to his cot returns, and, to the eager ears of wife and child, the simple story of his toil relates: what yield the furrow bears; and how the team the plover on the nest has spared; while Wat her courses ran; and speckled eggs in the warm hollow lay. Meanwhile the good wife on the table spreads her simple fare; and to the shepherd's flute, from toil released, the nymphs and swains join hands and foot it on the green. Then Eve lets down her sombre tresses brown and spreads her lucent veil o'er hamlet, spire, and mead, etc., etc. And the tune repeated itself once more.

The view repeated in its own way what the tune was saying. The sun was sinking; the colours were merging; and the view was saying how after toil men rest from their labours; how coolness comes; reason prevails; and having unharnessed the team from the plough, neighbours dig in cottage gardens and lean over cottage gates.

The cows, making a step forward, then standing still, were saying the same thing to perfection.

Folded in this triple melody, the audience sat gazing; and beheld gently and approvingly without interrogation, for it seemed inevitable, a box tree in a green tub take the place of the ladies' dressing-room; while on what seemed to be a wall, was hung a great clock face; the hands pointing to three minutes to the hour; which was seven.

Mrs Elmhurst roused herself from her reverie; and looked at her programme.

'Scene Two. The Mall,' she read out. 'Time; early morning. Enter Flavinda. Here she comes!'

Here came Millie Loder (shop assistant at Messrs Hunt and Dicksons, drapery emporium), in sprigged satin, representing Flavinda.

FLAV. *Seven he said, and there's the clock's word for it. But Valentine—where's Valentine? La! How my heart beats! Yet it's not the time o'day, for I'm often afoot before the sun's up in the meadows ... See—the fine folk passing! All a-tiptoeing like pea-cocks with spread tails! And I in my petticoat that looked so fine by my Aunt's cracked mirror. Why, here it's a dish clout ... And they heap their hair up*

like a birthday cake stuck about with candles ...
That's a diamond—that's a ruby ... Where's Valen-
tine? The Orange Tree in the Mall, he said. The*
tree—there. Valentine—nowhere. That's a courtier,
I'll warrant, that old fox with his tail between his legs.
That's a serving wench out without her master's
knowledge. That's a man with a broom to sweep paths
for the fine ladies' flounces ... La! the red in their
cheeks! They never got that in the fields, I warrant!
O faithless, cruel, hard-hearted Valentine. Valentine!
Valentine!

(She wrings her hands, turning from side to side.)

Didn't I leave my bed a-tiptoe and steal like a mouse
in the wainscot for fear of waking Aunt? And lard my
hair from her powder box? And scrub my cheeks to
make 'em shine? And lie awake watching the stars
climb the chimney pots? And give my gold guinea that
Godfather hid behind the mistletoe last Twelfth Night
to Deb so she shouldn't tell on me? And grease the
key in the lock so that Aunt shouldn't wake and shriek
Flavvy! Flavvy! Val, I say Val——That's him coming
... No, I could tell him a mile off the way he strides
the waves like what d'you call him in the picture book
... That's not Val ... That's a cit; that's a fop; raising
his glass, prithee, to have his fill of me ... I'll be home
then ... No, I won't ... That's to play the green girl
again and sew samplers ... I'm of age, ain't I, come
Michaelmas? Only three turns of the moon and I

[122]

inherit . . . Didn't I read it in the Will the day the ball
bounced on top of the old chest where Aunt keeps her
furbelows, and the lid opened? . . . 'All I die possessed
of to my Daughter . . .' So far I'd read when the old
lady came tapping down the passage like a blind man
in an alley . . . I'm no castaway, I'd have you know,
Sir; no fishtail mermaid with a robe of seaweed, at
your mercy. I'm a match for any of 'em—the chits
you dally with, and bid me meet you at the Orange
Tree when you're drowsing the night off spent in their
arms . . . Fie upon you, Sir, making sport with a poor
girl so . . . I'll not cry, I swear I won't. I'll not brew a
drop of the salt liquid for a man who's served me so
. . . Yet to think on't—how we hid in the dairy the
day the cat jumped. And read romances under the
holly tree. La! how I cried when the Duke left poor
Polly . . . And my Aunt found me with eyes like red
jellies. 'What stung, niece?' says she. And cried 'Quick
Deb, the blue bag.' I told ye . . . La, to think I read it
all in a book and cried for another! . . . Hist, what's
there among the trees? It's come—it's gone. The
breeze is it? In the shade now—in the sun now . . .
Valentine on my life! It's he! Quick, I'll hide. Let the
tree conceal me!

(Flavinda hides behind the tree.)

He's here . . . He turns . . . He casts about . . . He's
lost the scent . . . He gazes—this way, that way . . .
Let him feast his eyes on the fine faces—taste 'em,

sample 'em, say: 'That's the fine lady I danced with
. . . that I lay with . . . that I kissed under the mistletoe
. . .' Ha! How he spews 'em out! Brave Valentine!
How he casts his eyes upon the ground! How his
frowns become him! 'Where's Flavinda?' he sighs.
'She I love like the heart in my breast.' See him pull
his watch out! 'O faithless wretch!' he sighs. See how
he stamps the earth! Now turns on his heel . . . He
sees me—no, the sun's in his eyes. Tears fill 'em . . .
Lord, how he fingers his sword! He'll run it through
his breast like the Duke in the story book! . . . Stop,
Sir, stop!

(She reveals herself)

VALENTINE . . . *O Flavinda, O!*
FLAVINDA . . . *O Valentine, O!*

(They embrace)
The clock strikes nine.

'All that fuss about nothing!' a voice exclaimed.
People laughed. The voice stopped. But the voice had
seen; the voice had heard. For a moment Miss La
Trobe behind her tree glowed with glory. The next,
turning to the villagers who were passing in and out
between the trees, she barked:
'Louder! Louder!'
For the stage was empty; the emotion must be
continued; the only thing to continue the emotion
was the song and the words were inaudible.

'Louder! Louder!' She threatened them with her clenched fists.

Digging and delving (they sang), *hedging and ditching, we pass . . . Summer and winter, autumn and spring return . . . All passes but we, all changes . . . but we remain forever the same . . .* (the breeze blew gaps between their words).

'Louder, louder!' Miss La Trobe vociferated.

Palaces tumble down (they resumed), *Babylon, Nineveh, Troy . . . And Cæsar's great house . . . all fallen they lie . . . Where the plover nests was the arch . . . through which the Romans trod . . . Digging and delving we break with the share of the plough the clod . . . Where Clytemnestra watched for her Lord . . . saw the beacons blaze on the hills . . . we see only the clod . . . Digging and delving we pass . . . and the Queen and the Watch Tower fall . . . for Agamemnon has ridden away . . . Clytemnestra* is nothing but . . .*

The words died away. Only a few great names—Babylon, Nineveh, Clytemnestra, Agamemnon, Troy—floated across the open space. Then the wind rose, and in the rustle of the leaves even the great words became inaudible; and the audience sat staring at the villagers, whose mouths opened, but no sound came.

And the stage was empty. Miss La Trobe leant against the tree, paralysed. Her power had left her.

Beads of perspiration broke on her forehead. Illusion had failed. 'This is death,' she murmured, 'death.'

Then suddenly, as the illusion petered out, the cows took up the burden. One had lost her calf. In the very nick of time she lifted her great moon-eyed head and bellowed. All the great moon-eyed heads laid themselves back. From cow after cow came the same yearning bellow. The whole world was filled with dumb yearning. It was the primeval voice sounding loud in the ear of the present moment. Then the whole herd caught the infection. Lashing their tails, blobbed like pokers, they tossed their heads high, plunged and bellowed, as if Eros had planted his dart in their flanks and goaded them to fury. The cows annihilated the gap; bridged the distance; filled the emptiness and continued the emotion.

Miss La Trobe waved her hand ecstatically at the cows.

'Thank Heaven!' she exclaimed.

Suddenly the cows stopped; lowered their heads, and began browsing. Simultaneously the audience lowered their heads and read their programmes.

'The producer', Mrs Elmhurst read out for her husband's benefit, 'craves the indulgence of the audience. Owing to lack of time a scene has been omitted; and she begs the audience to imagine that in the interval Sir Spaniel Lilyliver has contracted an engagement with Flavinda; who had been about to plight her troth; when Valentine, hidden inside the grand-

father's clock, steps forward; claims Flavinda as his
bride; reveals the plot to rob her of her inheritance;
and during the confusion that ensues, the lovers fly
together, leaving Lady Harpy and Sir Spaniel alone
together.'

'We're asked to imagine all that,' she said, putting
down her glasses.

'That's very wise of her,' said Mrs Manresa,
addressing Mrs Swithin. 'If she'd put it all in, we
should have been here till midnight. So we've got to
imagine, Mrs Swithin.' She patted the old lady on the
knee.

'Imagine?' said Mrs Swithin. 'How right! Actors
show us too much. The Chinese, you know, put a
dagger on the table and that's a battle. And so
Racine* . . .'

'Yes, they bore one stiff,' Mrs Manresa interrupted,
scenting culture, resenting the snub to the jolly
human heart. 'T'other day I took my nephew—such
a jolly boy at Sandhurst*—to *Pop Goes the Weasel*.
Seen it?' She turned to Giles.

'Up and down the City Road,' he hummed by way
of an answer.

'Did your Nanny sing that!' Mrs Manresa
exclaimed. 'Mine did. And when she said "Pop" she
made a noise like a cork being drawn from a ginger-
beer bottle. Pop!'

She made the noise.

'Hush, hush,' someone whispered.

'Now I'm being naughty and shocking your aunt,' she said. 'We must be good and attend. This is Scene Three. Lady Harpy Harraden's Closet. The sound of horses' hooves is heard in the distance.'

The sound of horses' hooves, energetically represented by Albert the idiot with a wooden spoon on a tray, died away.

LADY H.H. *Half-way to Gretna Green* already! O my deceitful niece! You that I rescued from the brine and stood on the hearthstone dripping! O that the whale had swallowed you whole! Perfidious porpoise, O! Didn't the Horn book teach you Honour thy Great Aunt? How have you misread it and misspelt it, learnt thieving and cheating and reading of wills in old boxes and hiding of rascals in honest time-pieces that have never missed a second since King Charles's day! O Flavinda! O porpoise, O!*

SIR S.L. (trying to pull on his jack boots) *Old— old—old. He called me 'old'—'To your bed, old fool, and drink hot posset!'*

LADY H.H. *And she, stopping at the door and pointing the finger of scorn at me said 'old', Sir—'woman' Sir—I that am in the prime of life and a lady!*

SIR S.L. (tugging at his boots) *But I'll be even with him. I'll have the law on 'em! I'll run 'em to earth . . .*

(He hobbles up and down, one boot on, one boot off)

LADY H.H. (laying her hand on his arm) *Have mercy on your gout, Sir Spaniel. Bethink you, Sir—let's not run mad, we that are on the sunny side of fifty. What's this youth they prate on? Nothing but a goose feather blown on a north wind. Sit you down, Sir Spaniel. Rest your leg—so——*

(She pushes a cushion under his leg)

SIR S.L. *'Old' he called me . . . jumping from the clock like a jack-in-the-box . . . And she, making mock of me, points to my leg and cries 'Cupid's darts, Sir Spaniel, Cupid's darts.' O that I could braise 'em in a mortar and serve 'em up smoking hot on the altar of—O my gout, O my gout!*

LADY H.H. *This talk, Sir, ill befits a man of sense. Bethink you, Sir, only t'other day you were invoking—ahem—the Constellations. Cassiopeia, Aldebaran; the Aurora Borealis . . . It's not to be denied that one of 'em has left her sphere, has shot, has eloped, to put it plainly, with the entrails of a timepiece, the mere pendulum of a grandfather's clock. But, Sir Spaniel, there are some stars that—ahem—stay fixed; that shine, to put it in a nutshell, never so bright as by a sea-coal fire on a brisk morning.*

SIR S.L. *O that I were five and twenty with a sharp sword at my side!*

LADY H.H. (bridling) *I take your meaning, Sir. Te hee—To be sure, I regret it as you do. But youth's not all. To let you into a secret, I've passed the meridian*

[129]

myself. Am on t'other side of the Equator too. Sleep sound o' nights without turning. The dog days are over . . . But bethink you, Sir. Where there's a will there's a way.

SIR S.L. *God's truth Ma'am . . . ah my foot's like a burning, burning horseshoe on the devil's anvil, ah!—what's your meaning?*

LADY H.H. *My meaning, Sir? Must I disrupt my modesty and unquilt that which has been laid in lavender since, my lord, peace be to his name—'tis twenty years since—was lapped in lead? In plain words, Sir, Flavinda's flown. The cage is empty. But we that have bound our wrists with cowslips might join 'em with a stouter chain. To have done with fallals and figures. Here am I, Asphodilla—but my plain name Sue. No matter what my name is— Asphodilla or Sue—here am I, hale and hearty, at your service. Now that the plot's out, Brother Bob's bounty must go to the virgins. That's plain. Here's Lawyer Quill's word for it. 'Virgins . . . in perpetuity . . . sing for his soul.' And I warrant you, he has need of it . . . But no matter. Though we have thrown that to the fishes that might have wrapped us in lamb's-wool, I'm no beggar. There's messuages; tenements;* napery; cattle; my dowry; an inventory. I'll show you; engrossed on parchment; enough I'll warrant you to keep us handsomely, for what's to run of our time, as husband and wife.*

SIR S.L. *Husband and wife! So that's the plain truth*

of it! Why, Madam, I'd rather lash myself to a tar barrel, be bound to a thorn tree in a winter's gale. Faugh!

LADY H.H. ... *A tar barrel, quotha! A thorn tree—quotha! You that were harping on galaxies and milky ways! You that were swearing I outshone 'em all! A pox on you—you faithless! You shark, you! You serpent in jack boots, you! So you won't have me? Reject my hand do you?*

(She proffers her hand; he strikes it from him.)

SIR S.L. ... *Hide your chalk stones* in a woollen mit! pah! I'll none of 'em! Were they diamond, pure diamond and half the habitable globe and all its concubines strung in string round your throat I'd none of it ... none of it. Unhand me, scritch owl, witch, vampire! Let me go!*

LADY H.H. ... *So all your fine words were tinsel wrapped round a Christmas cracker!*

SIR S.L. ... *Bells hung on an ass's neck! Paper roses on a barber's pole ... O my foot, my foot ... Cupid's darts, she mocked me ... Old, old, he called me old ...*

(He hobbles away)

LADY H.H. (left alone) *All gone. Following the wind. He's gone; she's gone; and the old clock that the rascal made himself into a pendulum for is the only one of 'em all to stop. A pox on 'em—turning an*

*honest woman's house into a brothel. I that was
Aurora Borealis am shrunk to a tar barrel. I that was
Cassiopeia am turned to a she-ass. My head turns.
There's no trusting man nor woman; nor fine speeches;
nor fine looks. Off comes the sheep's skin; out creeps
the serpent. Get ye to Gretna Green; couch on the wet
grass and breed vipers. My head spins . . . Tar barrels,
quotha. Cassiopeia . . . Chalk stones . . . Andromeda
. . . Thorn trees . . . Deb, I say, Deb (She holloas)
Unlace me. I'm fit to burst . . . Bring me my green
baize table and set the cards . . . And my fur lined
slippers, Deb. And a dish of chocolate . . . I'll be even
with 'em . . . I'll outlive 'em all . . . Deb, I say! Deb!
A pox on the girl! Can't she hear me? Deb, I say, you
gipsy's spawn that I snatched from the hedge and
taught to sew samplers! Deb! Deb!*

(She throws open the door leading to the maid's
closet)

*Empty! She's gone too! . . . Hist, what's that on the
dresser?*

(She picks up a scrap of paper and reads)

*'What care I for your goose-feather bed? I'm off with
the raggle-taggle gipsies,* O! Signed: Deborah, one
time your maid.' So! She that I fed on apple parings
and crusts from my own table, she that I taught to
play cribbage and sew chemises . . . she's gone too. O
ingratitude, thy name is Deborah! Who's to wash the*

dishes now; who's to bring me my posset now, suffer my temper and unlace my stays? . . . All gone, I'm alone then. Sans niece, sans lover; and sans maid.

> *And so to end the play, the moral is,*
> *The God of love is full of tricks;*
> *Into the foot his dart he sticks,*
> *But the way of the will is plain to see;*
> *Let holy virgins hymn perpetually:*
> *'Where there's a will there's a way.'*
> *Good people all, farewell.*
> (dropping a curtsey, Lady H.H. withdrew)

The scene ended. Reason descended from her plinth. Gathering her robes about her, serenely acknowledging the applause of the audience, she passed across the stage; while Lords and Ladies in stars and garters followed after; Sir Spaniel limping escorted Lady Harraden smirking; and Valentine and Flavinda arm in arm bowed and curtsied.

'God's truth!' cried Bartholomew catching the infection of the language. 'There's a moral for you!'

He threw himself back in his chair and laughed, like a horse whinnying.

A moral. What? Giles supposed it was: Where there's a Will there's a Way. The words rose and pointed a finger of scorn at him. Off to Gretna Green with his girl; the deed done. Damn the consequences.

'Like to see the greenhouse?' he said abruptly, turning to Mrs Manresa.

'Love to!' she exclaimed, and rose.

[133]

Was there an interval? Yes, the programme said so. The machine in the bushes went chuff, chuff, chuff. And the next scene?

'The Victorian age,' Mrs Elmhurst read out. Presumably there was time then for a stroll round the gardens, even for a look over the house. Yet somehow they felt—how could one put it—a little not quite here or there. As if the play had jerked the ball out of the cup; as if what I call myself was still floating unattached, and didn't settle. Not quite themselves, they felt. Or was it simply that they felt clothes conscious? Skimpy out-of-date voile dresses; flannel trousers; panama hats; hats wreathed with raspberry-coloured net in the style of the Royal Duchess's hat at Ascot* seemed flimsy somehow.

'How lovely the clothes were,' said someone, casting a last look at Flavinda disappearing. 'Most becoming. I wish . . .'

Chuff, chuff, chuff went the machine in the bushes, accurately, insistently.

Clouds were passing across the sky. The weather looked a little unsettled. Hogben's Folly was for a moment ashen white. Then the sun struck the gilt vane of Bolney Minster.

'Looks a little unsettled,' said someone.

'Up you get . . . Let's stretch our legs,' said another voice. Soon the lawns were floating with little moving islands of coloured dresses. Yet some of the audience remained seated.

'Major and Mrs Mayhew,' Page the reporter noted, licking his pencil. As for the play, he would collar Miss Whatshername and ask for a synopsis. But Miss La Trobe had vanished.

Down among the bushes she worked like a nigger. Flavinda was in her petticoats. Reason had thrown her mantle on a holly hedge. Sir Spaniel was tugging at his jack boots. Miss La Trobe was scattering and foraging.

'The Victorian mantle with the bead fringe . . . Where is the damned thing? Chuck it here . . . Now the whiskers . . .'

Ducking up and down she cast her quick bird's eye over the bushes at the audience. The audience was on the move. The audience was strolling up and down. They kept their distance from the dressing-room; they respected the conventions. But if they wandered too far, if they began exploring the grounds, going over the house, then . . . Chuff, chuff, chuff went the machine. Time was passing. How long would time hold them together? It was a gamble; a risk . . . And she laid about her energetically, flinging clothes on the grass.

Over the tops of the bushes came stray voices, voices without bodies, symbolical voices they seemed to her, half hearing, seeing nothing, but still, over the bushes, feeling invisible threads connecting the bodi-less voices.

'It all looks very black.'

'No one wants it—save those damned Germans.'
There was a pause.
'I'd cut down those trees . . .'
'How they get their roses to grow!'
'They say there's been a garden here for five
hundred years . . .'
'Why even old Gladstone,* to do him justice . . .'
Then there was silence. The voices passed the
bushes. The trees rustled. Many eyes, Miss La Trobe
knew, for every cell in her body was absorbent,
looked at the view. Out of the corner of her eye she
could see Hogben's Folly; then the vane flashed.

'The glass is falling,' said a voice.

She could feel them slipping through her fingers,
looking at the view.

'Where's that damned woman, Mrs Rogers? Who's
seen Mrs Rogers?' she cried, snatching up a Victorian
mantle.

Then, ignoring the conventions, a head popped up
between the trembling sprays: Mrs Swithin's.

'Oh Miss La Trobe!' she exclaimed; and stopped.
Then she began again; 'Oh Miss La Trobe, I do
congratulate you!'

She hesitated. 'You've given me . . .' She skipped,
then alighted—'Ever since I was a child I've felt . . .'
A film fell over her eyes, shutting off the present. She
tried to recall her childhood; then gave it up; and,
with a little wave of her hand, as if asking Miss La
Trobe to help her out, continued: 'This daily round;

[136]

this going up and down stairs; this saying "What am I going for? My specs? I have 'em on my nose" . . .'

She gazed at Miss La Trobe with a cloudless old-aged stare. Their eyes met in a common effort to bring a common meaning to birth. They failed; and Mrs Swithin, laying hold desperately of a fraction of her meaning, said: 'What a small part I've had to play! But you've made me feel I could have played . . . Cleopatra!'

She nodded between the trembling bushes and ambled off.

The villagers winked. 'Batty' was the word for old Flimsy, breaking through the bushes.

'I might have been—Cleopatra,' Miss La Trobe repeated. 'You've stirred in me my unacted part,' she meant.

'Now for the skirt, Mrs Rogers,' she said.

Mrs Rogers stood grotesque in her black stockings. Miss La Trobe pulled the voluminous flounces of the Victorian age over her head. She tied the tapes. 'You've twitched the invisible strings,' was what the old lady meant; and revealed—of all people—Cleopatra! Glory possessed her. Ah, but she was not merely a twitcher of individual strings; she was one who seethes wandering bodies and floating voices in a cauldron, and makes rise up from its amorphous mass a recreated world. Her moment was on her—her glory.

'There!' she said, tying the black ribbons under

Mrs Rogers' chin. 'That's done it! Now for the gentleman. Hammond!'

She beckoned Hammond. Sheepishly he came forward, and submitted to the application of black side whiskers. With his eyes half shut, his head leant back, he looked, Miss La Trobe thought, like King Arthur—noble, knightly, thin.

'Where's the Major's old frock coat?' she asked, trusting to the effect of that to transform him.

Tick, tick, tick, the machine continued. Time was passing. The audience was wandering, dispersing. Only the tick tick of the gramophone held them together. There, sauntering solitary far away by the flower beds was Mrs Giles escaping.

'The tune!' Miss La Trobe commanded. 'Hurry up! The tune! The next tune! Number Ten!'

'Now may I pluck', Isa murmured, picking a rose, 'my single flower. The white or the pink? And press it so, twixt thumb and finger . . .'

She looked among the passing faces for the face of the man in grey. There he was for one second; but surrounded, inaccessible. And now vanished.

She dropped her flower. What single, separate leaf could she press? None. Nor stray by the beds alone. She must go on; and she turned in the direction of the stable.

'Where do I wander?' she mused. 'Down what

[138]

draughty tunnels? Where the eyeless wind blows?
And there grows nothing for the eye. No rose. To
issue where? In some harvestless dim field where no
evening lets fall her mantle; nor sun rises. All's equal
there. Unblowing, ungrowing are the roses there.
Change is not; nor the mutable and lovable; nor
greetings nor partings; nor furtive findings and feel-
ings, where hand seeks hand and eye seeks shelter
from the eye.'

She had come into the stable yard where the dogs
were chained; where the buckets stood; where the
great pear tree spread its ladder of branches against
the wall. The tree whose roots went beneath the flags,
was weighted with hard green pears. Fingering one of
them she murmured: 'How am I burdened with what
they drew from the earth; memories; possessions.
This is the burden that the past laid on me, last little
donkey in the long caravanserai crossing the desert.
"Kneel down," said the past. "Fill your pannier from
our tree. Rise up, donkey. Go your way till your
heels blister and your hoofs crack."'

The pear was hard as stone. She looked down at
the cracked flags beneath which the roots spread.
'That was the burden', she mused, 'laid on me in the
cradle; murmured by waves; breathed by restless elm
trees; crooned by singing women; what we must
remember; what we would forget.'

She looked up. The gilt hands of the stable clock

pointed inflexibly at two minutes to the hour. The clock was about to strike.

'Now comes the lightning,' she muttered, 'from the stone blue sky. The thongs are burst that the dead tied. Loosed are our possessions.'

Voices interrupted. People passed the stable yard, talking.

'It's a good day, some say, the day we are stripped naked. Others, it's the end of the day. They see the Inn and the Inn's keeper. But none speaks with a single voice. None with a voice free from the old vibrations. Always I hear corrupt murmurs; the chink of gold and metal. Mad music . . .'

More voices sounded. The audience was streaming back to the terrace. She roused herself. She encouraged herself. 'On little donkey, patiently stumble. Hear not the frantic cries of the leaders who in that they seek to lead desert us. Nor the chatter of china faces glazed and hard. Hear rather the shepherd, coughing by the farmyard wall; the withered tree that sighs when the Rider gallops; the brawl in the barrack room when they stripped her naked; or the cry which in London when I thrust the window open someone cries . . .' She had come out on to the path that led past the greenhouse. The door was kicked open. Out came Mrs Manresa and Giles. Unseen, Isa followed them across the lawns to the front row of seats.

The chuff, chuff chuff, of the machine in the bushes had stopped. In obedience to Miss La Trobe's command, another tune had been put on the gramophone. Number Ten. London street cries it was called. 'A Pot Pourri.'

'Lavender, sweet lavender, who'll buy my sweet lavender' the tune trilled and tinkled, ineffectively shepherding the audience. Some ignored it. Some still wandered. Others stopped, but stood upright. Some, like Colonel and Mrs Mayhew, who had never left their seats, brooded over the blurred carbon sheet which had been issued for their information.

'The Nineteenth Century.' Colonel Mayhew did not dispute the producer's right to skip two hundred years in less than fifteen minutes. But the choice of scenes baffled him.

'Why leave out the British Army? What's history without the Army, eh?' he mused. Inclining her head, Mrs Mayhew protested after all one mustn't ask too much. Besides, very likely there would be a Grand Ensemble, round the Union Jack, to end with. Meanwhile, there was the view. They looked at the view.

'Sweet lavender . . . sweet lavender . . .' Humming the tune old Mrs Lynn Jones (of the Mount) pushed a chair forward. 'Here Etty,' she said, and plumped down, with Etty Springett, with whom, since both were widows now, she shared a house.

'I remember . . .' she nodded in time to the tune, 'You remember too—how they used to cry it down the streets.' They remembered—the curtains blowing, and the men crying: 'All a blowing, all a growing,' as they came with geraniums, sweet william, in pots, down the street.

'A harp, I remember, and a hansom and a growler.* So quiet the street was then. Two for a hansom, was it? One for a growler? And Ellen, in cap and apron, whistling in the street? D'you remember? And the runners, my dear, who followed, all the way from the station, if one had a box.'

The tune changed. 'Any old iron, any old iron to sell?' 'D'you remember? That was what the men shouted in the fog. Seven Dials* they came from. Men with red handkerchiefs. Garotters,* did we call them? You couldn't walk—O, dear me, no—home from the play. Regent Street. Piccadilly. Hyde Park Corner. The loose women . . . And everywhere loaves of bread in the gutter. The Irish you know round Covent Garden* . . . Coming back from a Ball, past the clock at Hyde Park Corner, d'you remember the feel of white gloves? . . . My father remembered the old Duke* in the Park.* Two fingers like that—he'd touch his hat . . . I've got my mother's album. A lake and two lovers. She'd copied out Byron, I suppose, in what was called then the Italian hand . . .'

'What's that? "Knocked 'em in the Old Kent Road."* I remember the bootboy whistled it. O, my dear, the servants . . . Old Ellen . . . Sixteen pound a year wages . . . And the cans of hot water! And the crinolines! And the stays! D'you remember the Crys-

tal Palace,* and the fireworks, and how Mira's slipper
got lost in the mud?'

'That's young Mrs Giles . . . I remember her
mother. She died in India . . . We wore, I suppose, a
great many petticoats then. Unhygienic? I dare say
. . . Well, look at my daughter. To the right, just
behind you. Forty, but slim as a wand. Each flat has
its refrigerator . . . It took my mother half the morning to order dinner . . . We were eleven. Counting
servants, eighteen in family . . . Now they simply ring
up the Stores . . . That's Giles coming, with Mrs
Manresa. She's a type I don't myself fancy. I may be
wrong . . . And Colonel Mayhew, as spruce as ever
. . . And Mr Cobbet of Cobbs Corner, there, under
the Monkey Puzzle Tree. One don't see him often
. . . That's what's so nice—it brings people together.
These days, when we're all so busy, that's what one
wants . . . The programme? Have you got it? Let's
see what comes next . . . The Nineteenth Century . . .
Look, there's the chorus, the villagers, coming on
now, between the trees. First, there's a prologue . . .'

A great box, draped in red baize festooned with
heavy gold tassels had been moved into the middle of
the stage. There was a swish of dresses, a stir of
chairs. The audience seated themselves, hastily, guiltily. Miss La Trobe's eye was on them. She gave them
ten seconds to settle their faces. Then she flicked her
hand. A pompous march tune brayed. 'Firm, elatant,
bold and blatant,' etc. . . . And once more a huge

symbolical figure emerged from the bushes. It was Budge the publican; but so disguised that even cronies who drank with him nightly failed to recognize him; and a little titter of enquiry as to his identity ran about among the villagers. He wore a long black many-caped cloak; waterproof; shiny; of the substance of a statue in Parliament Square;* a helmet which suggested a policeman; a row of medals crossed his breast; and in his right hand he held extended a special constable's baton (loaned by Mr Willert of the Hall). It was his voice, husky and rusty, issuing from a thick black cotton-wool beard that gave him away.

'Budge, Budge. That's Mr Budge,' the audience whispered.

Budge extended his truncheon and spoke:

It ain't an easy job, directing the traffic at 'Yde Park Corner. Buses and 'ansom cabs. All a-clatter on the cobbles. Keep to the right, can't you? Hi there, stop!

(He waved his truncheon)

There she goes, the old party with the umbrella right under the 'orse's nose.

(The truncheon pointed markedly at Mrs Swithin)

She raised her skinny hand as if in truth she had fluttered off the pavement on the impulse of the moment to the just rage of authority. Got her, Giles thought, taking sides with authority against his aunt.

Fog or fine weather, I does my duty (Budge continued). *At Piccadilly Circus; at 'Yde Park Corner, directing the traffic of 'Er Majesty's Empire. The Shah of Persia; Sultan of Morocco; or it may be 'Er Majesty in person; or Cook's tourists; black men; white men; sailors, soldiers; crossing the ocean; to proclaim her Empire; all of 'em Obey the Rule of my truncheon.*

(He flourished it magnificently from right to left)

But my job don't end there. I take under my protection and direction the purity and security of all Her Majesty's minions; in all parts of her dominions; insist that they obey the laws of God and Man.

The laws of God and Man (he repeated and made as if to consult a Statute, engrossed on a sheet of parchment which with great deliberation he now produced from his trouser pocket)

Go to Church on Sunday; on Monday, nine sharp, catch the City Bus. On Tuesday it may be, attend a meeting at the Mansion House* for the redemption of the sinner; at dinner on Wednesday attend another—turtle soup. Some bother it may be in Ireland; Famine. Fenians.* What not. On Thursday it's the natives of Peru require protection and correction; we give 'em what's due. But mark you, our rule don't end there. It's a Christian country, our Empire; under the White

Queen Victoria. Over thought and religion; drink;
dress; manners; marriage too, I wield my truncheon.
Prosperity and respectability always go, as we know,
'and in 'and. The ruler of an Empire must keep his
eye on the cot; spy too in the kitchen; drawing-room;
library; wherever one or two, me and you, come
together. Purity our watchword; prosperity and
respectability. If not, why, let 'em fester in . . .

(He paused—no, he had not forgotten his
words)

*Cripplegate; St Giles's; Whitechapel; the Minories.**
Let 'em sweat at the mines; cough at the looms;
rightly endure their lot. That's the price of Empire;
that's the white man's burden. And, I can tell you, to
direct the traffic orderly, at 'Yde Park Corner, Picca-
dilly Circus, is a whole-time, white man's job.

He paused, eminent, dominant, glaring from his
pedestal. A very fine figure of a man he was, everyone
agreed, his truncheon extended; his waterproof pendant. It only wanted a shower of rain, a flight of
pigeons round his head, and the pealing bells of St
Paul's and the Abbey* to transform him into the very
spit and image of a Victorian constable; and to
transport them to a foggy London afternoon, with
the muffin bells ringing and the church bells pealing
at the very height of Victorian prosperity.

There was a pause. The voices of the pilgrims singing, as they wound in and out between the trees, could be heard; but the words were inaudible. The audience sat waiting.

'Tut-tut-tut,' Mrs Lynn Jones expostulated. 'There were grand men among them . . .' Why she did not know, yet somehow she felt that a sneer had been aimed at her father; therefore at herself.

Etty Springett tutted too. Yet, children did draw trucks in mines; there was the basement; yet Papa read Walter Scott aloud after dinner; and divorced ladies were not received at Court. How difficult to come to any conclusion! She wished they would hurry on with the next scene. She liked to leave a theatre knowing exactly what was meant. Of course this was only a village play . . . They were setting another scene, round the red baize box. She read out from her programme:

'The Picnic Party. About 1860. Scene: A Lake. Characters——'

She stopped. A sheet had been spread on the Terrace. It was a lake apparently. Roughly painted ripples represented water. Those green stakes were bulrushes. Rather prettily, real swallows darted across the sheet.

'Look, Minnie!' she exclaimed. 'Those are real swallows!'

'Hush, hush,' she was admonished. For the scene had begun. A young man in peg-top trousers and side whiskers carrying a spiked stick appeared by the lake.

EDGAR T. . . . *Let me help you, Miss Hardcastle! There!*

(he helps Miss Eleanor Hardcastle, a young lady in crinoline and mushroom hat to the top. They stand for a moment panting slightly, looking at the view.)

ELEANOR. *How small the Church looks down among the trees!*

EDGAR . . . *So this is Wanderer's Well, the trysting place.*

ELEANOR . . . *Please Mr Thorold, finish what you were saying before the others come. You were saying, 'Our aim in life . . .'*

EDGAR . . . *Should be to help our fellow men.*

ELEANOR (sighing deeply). *How true—how profoundly true!*

EDGAR . . . *Why sigh, Miss Hardcastle?—You have nothing to reproach yourself with—you whose whole life is spent in the service of others. It was of myself that I was thinking. I am no longer young. At twenty-four the best days of life are over. My life has passed* (he throws a pebble on to the lake) *like a ripple in water.*

ELEANOR. *Oh Mr Thorold, you do not know me. I am not what I seem. I too—*

EDGAR . . . *Do not tell me, Miss Hardcastle—no, I cannot believe it—You have doubted?*

ELEANOR. *Thank Heaven not that, not that . . . But safe and sheltered as I am, always at home, protected as you see me, as you think me. O what am I saying? But yes, I will speak the truth, before Mama comes. I too have longed to convert the heathen!*

EDGAR . . . *Miss Hardcastle . . . Eleanor . . . You tempt me! Dare I ask you? No—so young, so fair, so innocent. Think, I implore you, before you answer.*

ELEANOR . . . *I have thought—on my knees!*

EDGAR (taking a ring from his pocket) *Then . . . My mother with her last breath charged me to give this ring only to one to whom a lifetime in the African desert among the heathens would be——*

ELEANOR (taking the ring) *Perfect happiness! But hist!* (She slips the ring into her pocket) *Here's Mama!* (They start asunder)

(Enter Mrs Hardcastle, a stout lady in black bombazine, upon a donkey, escorted by an elderly gentleman in a deer-stalker's cap)

MRS H. . . . *So you stole a march upon us, young people. There was a time, Sir John, when you and I were always first on top. Now. . .*

(He helps her to alight. Children, young men, young women, some carrying hampers, others butterfly nets, others spy-glasses, others tin botanical cases arrive. A rug is thrown by the lake and Mrs H. and Sir John seat themselves on camp stools.)

MRS H. ... *Now who'll fill the kettles? Who'll gather the sticks? Alfred* (to a small boy), *don't run about chasing butterflies or you'll make yourself sick ... Sir John and I will unpack the hampers, here where the grass is burnt, where we had the picnic last year.*

(The young people scatter off in different directions. Mrs H. And Sir John begin to unpack the hamper)

MRS H. ... *Last year poor dear Mr Beach was with us. It was a blessed release* (She takes out a black-bordered handkerchief and wipes her eyes). *Every year one of us is missing. That's the ham ... That's the grouse ... There in that packet are the game pasties ...* (She spreads the eatables on the grass) *As I was saying poor dear Mr Beach ... I do hope the cream hasn't curdled. Mr Hardcastle is bringing the claret. I always leave that to him. Only when Mr Hardcastle gets talking with Mr Pigott about the Romans ... last year they quite came to words ... But it's nice for gentlemen to have a hobby, though they do gather the dust—those skulls and things ... But I was saying——poor dear Mr Beach ... I*

[150]

wanted to ask you (she drops her voice) *as a friend of the family, about the new clergyman—they can't hear us, can they? No, they're picking up sticks ... Last year, such a disappointment. Just got the things out ... down came the rain. But I wanted to ask you, about the new clergyman, the one who's come in place of dear Mr Beach. I'm told the name's Sibthorp. To be sure, I hope I'm right, for I had a cousin who married a girl of that name, and as a friend of the family, we don't stand on ceremony ... And when one has daughters—I'm sure I quite envy you, with only one daughter, Sir John, and I have four! So I was asking you to tell me in confidence, about this young—if that's-his-name—Sibthorp, for I must tell you the day before yesterday our Mrs Potts happened to say, as she passed the Rectory, bringing our laundry, they were unpacking the furniture; and what did she see on top of the wardrobe? A tea cosy! But of course she might be mistaken ... But it occurred to me to ask you, as a friend of the family, in confidence,* has Mr Sibthorp a wife?

Here a chorus composed of villagers in Victorian mantles, side whiskers and top hats sang in concert:

O has Mr Sibthorp a wife? O has Mr Sibthorp a wife? That is the hornet, the bee in the bonnet, the screw in the cork and the drill; that whirling and twirling are for ever unfurling the folds of the motherly heart; for a mother must ask, if daughters she has, begot in the feathery billowy fourposter

[151]

*family bed, O did he unpack, with his prayer book
and bands; his gown and his cane; his rod and his
line; and the family album and gun; did he also
display the connubial respectable tea-table token, a
cosy with honeysuckle embossed. Has Mr Sibthorp a
wife? O has Mr Sibthorp a wife?*

While the chorus was sung, the picnickers assembled. Corks popped. Grouse, ham, chickens were
sliced. Lips munched. Glasses were drained. Nothing
was heard but the chump of jaws and the chink of
glasses.

'They did eat,' Mrs Lynn Jones whispered to Mrs
Springett. 'That's true. More than was good for them,
I dare say.'

MR HARDCASTLE . . . (brushing flakes of meat from
his whiskers) *Now . . .*

'Now what?' whispered Mrs Springett, anticipating
further travesty.

*Now that we have gratified the inner man, let us
gratify the desire of the spirit. I call upon one of the
young ladies for a song.*

CHORUS OF YOUNG LADIES . . . *O not me . . . not
me . . . I really couldn't . . . No, you cruel thing, you
know I've lost my voice . . . I can't sing without the
instrument . . . etc., etc.*

CHORUS OF YOUNG MEN. *O bosh! Let's have 'The
Last Rose of Summer'.* Let's have 'I never loved a
Dear Gazelle'.**

[152]

Mrs H. (authoritatively) *Eleanor and Mildred will now sing 'I'd be a Butterfly'.*

(Eleanor and Mildred rise obediently and sing a duet: 'I'd be a Butterfly'.)

Mrs H. *Thank you very much, my dears. And now gentlemen, Our Country!*

(Arthur and Edgar sing 'Rule Britannia'.)

Mrs H. . . . *Thank you very much. Mr Hardcastle*——

Mr Hardcastle (rising to his feet, clasping his fossil) *Let us pray.*

(the whole company rise to their feet)

'This is too much, too much,' Mrs Springett protested.

Mr H. . . . *Almighty God, giver of all good things, we thank Thee; for our food and drink; for the beauties of Nature; for the understanding with which Thou hast enlightened us* (he fumbled with his fossil) *And for thy great gift of Peace. Grant us to be thy servants on earth; grant us to spread the light of thy* . . .

Here the hindquarters of the donkey, represented by Albert the idiot, became active. Intentional was it, or accidental? 'Look at the donkey! Look at the donkey!' A titter drowned Mr Hardcastle's prayer; and then he was heard saying:

[153]

*. . . a happy homecoming with bodies refreshed by
thy bounty, and minds inspired by thy wisdom. Amen.*

Holding his fossil in front of him, Mr Hardcastle
marched off. The donkey was captured; hampers
were loaded; and forming into a procession, the
picnickers began to disappear over the hill.

EDGAR (winding up the procession with Eleanor)
To convert the heathen!

ELEANOR. *To help our fellow men!*

(The actors disappeared into the bushes.)

BUDGE . . . *It's time, gentlemen, time ladies, time
to pack up and be gone. From where I stand, truncheon in hand, guarding respectability, and prosperity,
and the purity of Victoria's land, I see before me*—(he
pointed: there was Pointz Hall; the rooks cawing; the
smoke rising)

'Ome, Sweet 'Ome

The gramophone took up the strain: *Through
pleasures and palaces, etc. There's no place like Home.*

BUDGE . . . *Home, gentlemen; home, ladies, it's
time to pack up and go home. Don't I see the fire* (he
pointed: one window blazed red) *blazing ever higher?
In kitchen; and nursery; drawing-room and library?
That's the fire of 'Ome. And see! Our Jane has
brought the tea. Now children where's the toys?
Mama, your knitting, quick. For here* (he swept his
truncheon at Cobbet of Cobbs Corner) *comes the
bread-winner, home from the city, home from the*

counter, home from the shop. 'Mama, a cup o' tea.'
'Children, gather round my knee. I will read aloud.
Which shall it be? Sinbad the sailor? Or some simple
tale from the Scriptures? And show you the pictures?
What none of 'em? Then out with the bricks. Let's
build: A conservatory. A laboratory? A mechanics'
institute?* Or shall it be a tower; with our flag on
top; where our widowed Queen, after tea, calls the
Royal orphans round her knee? For it's 'Ome, ladies,
'Ome, gentlemen. Be it never so humble, there's no
place like 'Ome.'

The gramophone warbled Home, Sweet Home,
and Budge, swaying slightly, descended from his box
and followed the procession off the stage.

There was an interval.

'Oh but it was beautiful,' Mrs Lynn Jones protested. Home she meant; the lamplit room; the ruby
curtains; and Papa reading aloud.

They were rolling up the lake and uprooting the
bulrushes. Real swallows were skimming over real
grass. But she still saw the home.

'It was . . .' she repeated, referring to the home.

'Cheap and nasty, I call it,' snapped Etty Springett,
referring to the play, and shot a vicious glance at
Dodge's green trousers, yellow spotted tie, and
unbuttoned waistcoat.

But Mrs Lynn Jones still saw the home. Was there,

she mused, as Budge's red baize pediment was rolled off, something—not impure, that wasn't the word—but perhaps 'unhygienic' about the home? Like a bit of meat gone sour, with whiskers, as the servants called it? Or why had it perished? Time went on and on like the hands of the kitchen clock. (The machine chuffed in the bushes.) If they had met with no resistance, she mused, nothing wrong, they'd still be going round and round and round. The Home would have remained; and Papa's beard, she thought, would have grown and grown; and Mama's knitting—what did she do with all her knitting?—Change had to come, she said to herself, or there'd have been yards and yards of Papa's beard, of Mama's knitting. Nowadays her son-in-law was clean shaven. Her daughter had a refrigerator ... Dear, how my mind wanders, she checked herself. What she meant was, change had to come, unless things were perfect; in which case she supposed they resisted Time. Heaven was changeless.

'Were they like that?' Isa asked abruptly. She looked at Mrs Swithin as if she had been a dinosaur or a very diminutive mammoth. Extinct she must be, since she had lived in the reign of Queen Victoria.

Tick, tick, tick, went the machine in the bushes.

'The Victorians,' Mrs Swithin mused. 'I don't believe' she said with her odd little smile, 'that there ever were such people. Only you and me and William dressed differently.'

'You don't believe in history,' said William.

[156]

The stage remained empty. The cows moved in the field. The shadows were deeper under the trees.

Mrs Swithin caressed her cross. She gazed vaguely at the view. She was off, they guessed, on a circular tour of the imagination—one-making. Sheep, cows, grass, trees, ourselves—all are one. If discordant, producing harmony—if not to us, to a gigantic ear attached to a gigantic head. And thus—she was smiling benignly—the agony of the particular sheep, cow, or human being is necessary; and so—she was beaming seraphically at the gilt vane in the distance—we reach the conclusion that *all* is harmony, could we hear it. And we shall. Her eyes now rested on the white summit of a cloud. Well, if the thought gave her comfort, William and Isa smiled across her, let her think it.

Tick tick tick the machine reiterated.

'D'you get her meaning?' said Mrs Swithin alighting suddenly. 'Miss La Trobe's?'

Isa, whose eyes had been wandering, shook her head.

'But you might say the same of Shakespeare,' said Mrs Swithin.

'Shakespeare and the musical glasses!'* Mrs Manresa intervened. 'Dear, what a barbarian you all make me feel!'

She turned to Giles. She invoked his help against this attack upon the jolly human heart.

'Tosh,' Giles muttered.

Nothing whatever appeared on the stage.

Darts of red and green light flashed from the rings on Mrs Manresa's fingers. He looked from them at Aunt Lucy. From her to William Dodge. From him to Isa. She refused to meet his eyes. And he looked down at his blood-stained tennis shoes.

He said (without words) 'I'm damnably unhappy.'

'So am I,' Dodge echoed.

'And I too,' Isa thought.

They were all caught and caged; prisoners; watching a spectacle. Nothing happened. The tick of the machine was maddening.

'On, little donkey' Isa murmured, 'crossing the desert . . . bearing your burden . . .'

She felt Dodge's eye upon her as her lips moved. Always some cold eye crawled over the surface like a winter blue-bottle! She flicked him off.

'What a time they take!' she exclaimed irritably.

'Another interval,' Dodge read out, looking at the programme.

'And after that, what?' asked Lucy.

'Present time. Ourselves,' he read.

'Let's hope to God that's the end,' said Giles gruffly.

'Now you're being naughty,' Mrs Manresa reproved her little boy, her surly hero.

No one moved. There they sat, facing the empty stage, the cows, the meadows and the view, while the machine ticked in the bushes.

'What's the object', said Bartholomew, suddenly rousing himself, 'of this entertainment?'

'The profits', Isa read out from her blurred carbon copy, 'are to go to a fund for installing electric light in the Church.'

'All our village festivals', Mr Oliver snorted turning to Mrs Manresa, 'end with a demand for money.'

'Of course, of course,' she murmured, deprecating his severity, and the coins in her bead bag jingled.

'Nothing's done for nothing in England,' the old man continued. Mrs Manresa protested. It might be true, perhaps, of the Victorians; but surely not of ourselves? Did she really believe that we were disinterested? Mr Oliver demanded.

'Oh you don't know my husband!' the wild child exclaimed, striking an attitude.

Admirable woman! You could trust her to crow when the hour struck like an alarm clock; to stop like an old bus horse when the bell rang. Oliver said nothing. Mrs Manresa had out her mirror and attended to her face.

All their nerves were on edge. They sat exposed. The machine ticked. There was no music. The horns of cars on the high road were heard. And the swish of trees. They were neither one thing nor the other; neither Victorians nor themselves. They were suspended, without being, in limbo. Tick, tick, tick went the machine.

Isa fidgeted; glancing to right and to left over her shoulder.

'Four and twenty blackbirds, strung upon a string,' she muttered.

'Down came an Ostrich, an eagle, an executioner. "Which of you is ripe," he said, "to bake in my pie?

Which of you is ripe, which of you is ready,

Come my pretty gentleman,

Come my pretty lady" . . .'

How long was she going to keep them waiting? 'The present time. Ourselves.' They read it on the programme. Then they read what came next: 'The profits are to go to a fund for installing electric light in the Church.' Where was the Church? Over there. You could see the spire among the trees.

'Ourselves . . .' They returned to the programme. But what could she know about ourselves? The Elizabethans yes; the Victorians, perhaps; but ourselves; sitting here on a June day in 1939—it was ridiculous. 'Myself'—it was impossible. Other people, perhaps . . . Cobbet of Cobbs Corner; the Major; old Bartholomew; Mrs Swithin—them, perhaps. But she won't get me—no, not me. The audience fidgeted. Sounds of laughter came from the bushes. But nothing whatsoever appeared on the stage.

'What's she keeping us waiting for?' Colonel

Mayhew asked irritably. 'They don't need to dress up if it's present time.'

Mrs Mayhew agreed. Unless of course she was going to end with a Grand Ensemble. Army; Navy; Union Jack; and behind them perhaps—Mrs Mayhew sketched what she would have done had it been her pageant—the Church. In cardboard. One window, looking east, brilliantly illuminated to symbolize— she could work that out when the time came.

'There she is, behind the tree,' she whispered, pointing at Miss La Trobe.

Miss La Trobe stood there with her eyes on her script. 'After Vic.' she had written, 'try ten mins. of present time. Swallows, cows, etc.' She wanted to expose them, as it were, to douche them, with present-time reality. But something was going wrong with the experiment. 'Reality too strong,' she muttered. 'Curse 'em!' She felt everything they felt. Audiences were the devil. O to write a play without an audience—*the* play. But here she was fronting her audience. Every second they were slipping the noose. Her little game had gone wrong. If only she'd a back-cloth to hang between the trees—to shut out cows, swallows, present time! But she had nothing. She had forbidden music. Grating her fingers in the bark, she damned the audience. Panic seized her. Blood seemed to pour from her shoes. This is death, death, death, she noted in the margin of her mind; when illusion fails. Unable to lift her hand, she stood facing the audience.

And then the shower fell, sudden, profuse.

No one had seen the cloud coming. There it was, black, swollen, on top of them. Down it poured like all the people in the world weeping. Tears, Tears. Tears.

'O that our human pain could here have ending!' Isa murmured. Looking up she received two great blots of rain full in her face. They trickled down her cheeks as if they were her own tears. But they were all people's tears, weeping for all people. Hands were raised. Here and there a parasol opened. The rain was sudden and universal. Then it stopped. From the grass rose a fresh earthy smell.

'That's done it,' sighed Miss La Trobe, wiping away the drops on her cheeks. Nature once more had taken her part. The risk she had run acting in the open air was justified. She brandished her script. Music began—A.B.C.—A.B.C. The tune was as simple as could be. But now that the shower had fallen, it was the other voice speaking, the voice that was no one's voice. And the voice that wept for human pain unending said:

> *The King is in his counting house,*
> *Counting out his money.*
> *The Queen is in her parlour . . .*

'O that my life could here have ending,' Isa murmured (taking care not to move her lips). Readily would she endow this voice with all her treasure if so be tears could be ended. The little twist of sound could have the whole of her. On the altar of the rain-soaked earth she laid down her sacrifice . . .

'O look!' she cried aloud.

That was a ladder. And that (a cloth roughly painted) was a wall. And that a man with a hod on his back. Mr Page the reporter, licking his pencil, noted: 'With the very limited means at her disposal, Miss La Trobe conveyed to the audience Civilization (the wall) in ruins; rebuilt (witness man with hod) by human effort; witness also woman handing bricks. Any fool could grasp that. Now issued black man in fuzzy wig; coffee-coloured ditto in silver turban; they signify presumably the League of . . .'*

A burst of applause greeted this flattering tribute to ourselves. Crude of course. But then she had to keep expenses down. A painted cloth must convey—what *The Times* and *Telegraph* both said in their leaders that very morning.

The tune hummed:

> *The King is in his counting house,*
> *Counting out his money,*
> *The Queen is in her parlour*
> *Eating . . .*

Suddenly the tune stopped. The tune changed. A waltz, was it? Something half known, half not. The swallows danced it. Round and round, in and out they skimmed. Real swallows. Retreating and advancing. And the trees, O the trees, how gravely and sedately like senators in council, or the spaced pillars of some cathedral church ... Yes, they barred the music, and massed and hoarded; and prevented what was fluid from overflowing. The swallows—or martins were they?—The temple-haunting martins* who come, have always come ... Yes, perched on the wall, they seemed to foretell what after all *The Times* was saying yesterday. Homes will be built. Each flat with its refrigerator, in the crannied wall.* Each of us a free man; plates washed by machinery; not an aeroplane to vex us; all liberated; made whole ...

The tune changed; snapped; broke; jagged. Foxtrot was it? Jazz? Anyhow the rhythm kicked, reared, snapped short. What a jangle and a jingle! Well, with the means at her disposal, you can't ask too much. What a cackle, in a cacophony! Nothing ended. So abrupt. And corrupt. Such an outrage; such an insult; And not plain. Very up to date, all the same. What is her game? To disrupt? Jog and trot? Jerk and smirk? Put the finger to the nose? Squint and pry? Peak and spy? O the irreverence of the generation which is only momentarily—thanks be—'the young'. The young, who can't make, but only break; shiver into splinters the old vision; smash to atoms what was whole. What a cackle, what a rattle what a yaffle—as they call the woodpecker, the laughing bird that flits from tree to tree.

Look! Out they come, from the bushes—the riff-raff. Children? Imps—elves—demons. Holding what? Tin cans? Bedroom candlesticks? Old jars? My dear, that's the cheval glass from the Rectory! And the mirror—that I lent her. My mother's. Cracked. What's the notion? Anything that's bright enough to reflect, presumably, ourselves?

Ourselves! Ourselves!

Out they leapt, jerked, skipped. Flashing, dazzling, dancing, jumping. Now old Bart . . . he was caught. Now Manresa. Here a nose . . . There a skirt . . . Then trousers only . . . Now perhaps a face . . . Ourselves? But that's cruel. To snap us as we are, before we've had time to assume . . . And only, too, in parts . . . That's what's so distorting and upsetting and utterly unfair.

Mopping, mowing, whisking, frisking, the looking glasses darted, flashed, exposed. People in the back rows stood up to see the fun. Down they sat, caught themselves . . . What an awful show-up! Even for the old who, one might suppose, hadn't any longer any care about their faces . . . And Lord! the jangle and the din! The very cows joined in. Walloping, tail lashing, the reticence of nature was undone, and the barriers which should divide Man the Master from the Brute were dissolved. Then the dogs joined in. Excited by the uproar, scurrying and worrying, here they came! Look at them! And the hound, the Afghan hound . . . look at him!

[165]

Then once more, in the uproar which by this time
has passed quite beyond control, behold Miss
Whatshername behind the tree summoned from the
bushes—or was it *they* who broke away—Queen
Bess; Queen Anne; and the girl in the Mall; and the
Age of Reason; and Budge the policeman; here they
came. And the Pilgrims. And the lovers. And the
grandfather's clock. And the old man with a beard.
They all appeared. What's more, each declaimed some
phrase or fragment from their parts . . . *I am not* (said
one) *in my perfect mind** . . . Another, *Reason am I
. . . And I? I'm the old top hat . . . Home is the
hunter,* home from the hill . . . Home? Where the
miner sweats, and the maiden faith is rudely strum-
peted . . . Sweet and low;* sweet and low, wind of the
western sea . . . Is that a dagger* that I see before me?
. . . The owl hoots and the ivy mocks tap-tap-tapping
on the pane . . . Lady I love till I die, leave thy
chamber and come . . . Where the worm weaves its
winding sheet . . . I'd be a butterfly. I'd be a butterfly
. . . In thy will is our peace** . . . *Here, Papa, take
your book and read aloud . . . Hark, hark, the dogs
do bark and the beggars . . .*
It was the cheval glass that proved too heavy.
Young Bonthorp for all his muscle couldn't lug the
damned thing about any longer. He stopped. So did
they all—hand glasses, tin cans, scraps of scullery
glass, harness room glass, and heavily embossed silver
mirrors—all stopped. And the audience saw them-

selves, not whole by any means, but at any rate sitting still.

The hands of the clock had stopped at the present moment. It was now. Ourselves.

So that was her little game! To show us up, as we are, here and how. All shifted, preened, minced; hands were raised, legs shifted. Even Bart, even Lucy, turned away. All evaded or shaded themselves—save Mrs Manresa who, facing herself in the glass, used it as a glass; had out her mirror; powdered her nose; and moved one curl, disturbed by the breeze, to its place.

'Magnificent!' cried old Bartholomew. Alone she preserved unashamed her identity, and faced without blinking herself. Calmly she reddened her lips.

The mirror bearers squatted; malicious; observant; expectant; expository.

'That's them,' the back rows were tittering. 'Must we submit passively to this malignant indignity?' the front row demanded. Each turned ostensibly to say— O whatever came handy—to his neighbour. Each tried to shift an inch or two beyond the inquisitive insulting eye. Some made as if to go.

'The play's over, I take it,' muttered Colonel Mayhew, retrieving his hat. 'It's time . . .'

But before they had come to any common conclusion, a voice asserted itself. Whose voice it was no one knew. It came from the bushes—a megaphonic,

anonymous, loud-speaking affirmation. The voice
said:

Before we part, ladies and gentlemen, before we go
... (Those who had risen sat down) ... *let's talk in
words of one syllable, without larding, stuffing or
cant. Let's break the rhythm and forget the rhyme.
And calmly consider ourselves. Some bony. Some fat.*
(The glasses confirmed this.) *Liars most of us. Thieves
too.* (The glasses made no comment on that.) *The
poor are as bad as the rich are. Perhaps worse. Don't
hide among rags. Or let our cloth protect us. Or for
the matter of that book learning; or skilful practice on
pianos; or laying on of paint. Or presume there's
innocency in childhood. Consider the sheep. Or faith
in love. Consider the dogs. Or virtue in those that
have grown white hairs. Consider the gun slayers,
bomb droppers here or there. They do openly what we
do slyly. Take for example* (here the megaphone
adopted a colloquial, conversational tone) *Mr M's
bungalow. A view spoilt for ever. That's murder ...
Or Mrs E's lipstick and blood-red nails ... A tyrant,
remember, is half a slave. Item the vanity of Mr H.
the writer, scraping in the dunghill for sixpenny fame
... Then there's the amiable condescension of the lady
of the manor—the upper class manner. And buying
shares in the market to sell 'em ... O we're all the
same. Take myself now. Do I escape my own repro-
bation, simulating indignation, in the bush, among
the leaves? There's a rhyme, to suggest, in spite of*

*protestation and the desire for immolation, I too have
had some, what's called, education . . . Look at ourselves, ladies and gentlemen! Then at the wall; and
ask how's this wall, the great wall, which we call,
perhaps miscall, civilization, to be built by* (here the
mirrors flicked and flashed) *orts, scraps and fragments
like ourselves?*

*All the same here I change (by way of the rhyme
mark ye) to a loftier strain—there's something to be
said: for our kindness to the cat; note too in to-day's
paper 'Dearly loved by his wife'; and the impulse
which leads us—mark you, when no one's looking—
to the window at midnight to smell the bean. Or the
resolute refusal of some pimpled dirty little scrub in
sandals to sell his soul. There is such a thing—you
can't deny it. What? You can't descry it? All you can
see of yourselves in scraps, orts and fragments? Well
then listen to the gramophone affirming . . .*

A hitch occurred here. The records had been mixed.
Fox trot, Sweet lavender, Home Sweet Home, Rule
Britannia—sweating profusely, Jimmy, who had
charge of the music, threw them aside and fitted the
right one—was it Bach, Handel, Beethoven, Mozart
or nobody famous, but merely a traditional tune?
Anyhow, thank Heaven, it was somebody speaking
after the anonymous bray of the infernal megaphone.
Like quicksilver sliding, filings magnetized, the
distracted united. The tune began; the first note meant
a second; the second a third. Then down beneath a

force was born in opposition; then another. On
different levels they diverged. On different levels
ourselves went forward; flower gathering some on
the surface; others descending to wrestle with the
meaning; but all comprehending; all enlisted. The
whole population of the mind's immeasurable profundity came flocking; from the unprotected, the
unskinned; and dawn rose; and azure; from chaos
and cacophony measure; but not the melody of
surface sound alone controlled it; but also the warring
battle-plumed warriors straining asunder: To part?
No. Compelled from the ends of the horizon; recalled
from the edge of appalling crevasses; they crashed;
solved; united. And some relaxed their fingers; and
others uncrossed their legs.

Was that voice ourselves? Scraps, orts and fragments, are we, also, that? The voice died away.

As waves withdrawing uncover; as mist uplifting
reveals; so, raising their eyes (Mrs Manresa's were
wet; for an instant tears ravaged her powder) they
saw, as waters withdrawing leave visible a tramp's old
boot, a man in a clergyman's collar surreptitiously
mounting a soap-box.

'The Rev. G. W. Streatfield', the reporter licked his
pencil and noted 'then spoke . . .'

All gazed. What an intolerable constriction, con-
traction, and reduction to simplified absurdity he was
to be sure! Of all incongruous sights a clergyman in
the livery of his servitude to the summing up was the

most grotesque and entire. He opened his mouth. O Lord, protect and preserve us from words the defilers, from words the impure! What need have we of words to remind us? Must I be Thomas, you Jane?

As if a rook had hopped unseen to a prominent bald branch, he touched his collar and hemmed his preliminary croak. One fact mitigated the horror; his forefinger, raised in the customary manner, was stained with tobacco juice. He wasn't such a bad fellow; the Rev. G. W. Streatfield; a piece of traditional church furniture; a corner cupboard; or the top beam of a gate, fashioned by generations of village carpenters after some lost-in-the-mists-of-antiquity model.

He looked at the audience; then up at the sky. The whole lot of them, gentles and simples, felt embarrassed, for him, for themselves. There he stood their representative spokesman; their symbol; themselves; a butt, a clod, laughed at by looking-glasses; ignored by the cows, condemned by the clouds which continued their majestic rearrangement of the celestial landscape; an irrelevant forked stake in the flow and majesty of the summer silent world.

His first words (the breeze had risen; the leaves were rustling) were lost. Then he was heard saying: 'What.' To that word he added another 'Message'; and at last a whole sentence emerged; not comprehensible; say rather audible. 'What message', it

[171]

seemed he was asking, 'was our pageant meant to convey?'

They folded their hands in the traditional manner as if they were seated in church.

'I have been asking myself'—the words were repeated—'what meaning, or message, this pageant was meant to convey?'

If he didn't know, calling himself Reverend, also M.A., who after all could?

'As one of the audience,' he continued (words now put on meaning) 'I will offer, very humbly, for I am not a critic'—and he touched the white gate that enclosed his neck with a yellow forefinger—'my interpretation. No, that is too bold a word. The gifted lady . . .' He looked round. La Trobe was invisible. He continued: 'Speaking merely as one of the audience, I confess I was puzzled. For what reason, I asked, were we shown these scenes? Briefly, it is true. The means at our disposal this afternoon were limited. Still we were shown different groups. We were shown, unless I mistake, the effort renewed. A few were chosen; the many passed in the background. That surely we were shown. But again, were we not given to understand—am I too presumptuous? Am I treading, like angels,* where as a fool I should absent myself? To me at least it was indicated that we are members one of another. Each is part of the whole. Yes, that occurred to me, sitting among you in the audience. Did I not perceive Mr Hardcastle here' (he

pointed) 'at one time a Viking? And in Lady Harri-
dan—excuse me, if I get the names wrong—a Canterbury pilgrim? We act different parts; but are the
same. That I leave to you. Then again, as the play or
pageant proceeded, my attention was distracted. Perhaps that too was part of the producer's intention? I
thought I perceived that nature takes her part. Dare
we, I asked myself, limit life to ourselves? May we
not hold that there is a spirit that inspires, pervades
. . .' (the swallows were sweeping round him. They
seemed cognizant of his meaning. Then they swept
out of sight.) 'I leave that to you. I am not here to
explain. That role has not been assigned me. I speak
only as one of the audience, one of ourselves. I caught
myself too reflected, as it happened in my own mirror
. . .' (Laughter) 'Scraps, orts and fragments! Surely,
we should unite?'

'But' ('but' marked a new paragraph) 'I speak also
in another capacity. As Treasurer of the Fund. In
which capacity' (he consulted a sheet of paper) 'I am
glad to be able to tell you that a sum of thirty-six
pounds ten shillings and eightpence has been raised
by this afternoon's entertainment towards our object:
the illumination of our dear old church.'

'Applause,' the reporter reported.

Mr Streatfield paused. He listened. Did he hear
some distant music?

He continued: 'But there is still a deficit' (he
consulted his paper) 'of one hundred and seventy-five

[173]

pounds odd. So that each of us who has enjoyed this pageant has still an opp ...' The word was cut in two. A zoom severed it. Twelve aeroplanes in perfect formation like a flight of wild duck came overhead. *That* was the music. The audience gaped; the audience gazed. Then zoom became drone. The planes had passed.

'... portunity', Mr Streatfield continued, 'to make a contribution.' He signalled. Instantly collecting boxes were in operation. Hidden behind glasses they emerged. Coppers rattled. Silver jingled. But O what a pity—how creepy it made one feel! Here came Albert, the idiot, jingling his collecting box—an aluminium saucepan without a lid. You couldn't very well deny him, poor fellow. Shillings were dropped. He rattled and sniggered; chattered and jibbered. As Mrs Parker made her contribution—half a crown as it happened—she appealed to Mr Streatfield to exorcize this evil, to extend the protection of his cloth.

The good man contemplated the idiot benignly. His faith had room, he indicated, for him too. He too, Mr Streatfield appeared to be saying, is part of ourselves. But not a part we like to recognize, Mrs Springett added silently, dropping her sixpence.

Contemplating the idiot, Mr Streatfield had lost the thread of his discourse. His command over words seemed gone. He twiddled the cross on his watch-chain. Then his hand sought his trouser pocket. Surreptitiously he extracted a small silver box. It was plain to all that the natural desire of the natural man was overcoming him. He had no further use for words.

'And now,' he resumed, cuddling the pipe lighter in the palm of his hand, 'for the pleasantest part of my duty. To propose a vote of thanks to the gifted lady . . .' He looked round for an object corresponding to this description. None such was visible. '. . . who wishes it seems to remain anonymous.' He paused. 'And so . . .' He paused again.

It was an awkward moment. How to make an end? Whom to thank? Every sound in nature was painfully audible; the swish of the trees; the gulp of a cow; even the skim of the swallows over the grass could be heard. But no one spoke. Whom could they make responsible? Whom could they thank for their entertainment? Was there no one?

Then there was a scuffle behind the bush; a preliminary premonitory scratching. A needle scraped a disc; chuff, chuff chuff; then having found the rut, there was a roll and a flutter which portended *God* . . . (they all rose to their feet) *Save the King*.

Standing the audience faced the actors; who also stood with their collecting boxes quiescent, their looking-glasses hidden, and the robes of their various parts hanging stiff.

> *Happy and glorious,*
> *Long to reign over us*
> *God save the King*

[175]

The notes died away.

Was that the end? The actors were reluctant to go. They lingered; they mingled. There was Budge the policeman talking to old Queen Bess. And the Age of Reason hobnobbed with the foreparts of the donkey. And Mrs Hardcastle patted out the folds of her crinoline. And little England, still a child, sucked a peppermint drop out of a bag. Each still acted the unacted part conferred on them by their clothes. Beauty was on them. Beauty revealed them. Was it the light that did it?—the tender, the fading, the uninquisitive but searching light of evening that reveals depths in water and makes even the red brick bungalow radiant?

'Look,' the audience whispered, 'O look, look, look—' And once more they applauded; and the actors joined hands and bowed.

Old Mrs Lynn Jones, fumbling for her bag, sighed, 'What a pity—must they change?'

But it was time to pack up and be off.

'Home, gentlemen; home ladies; it's time to pack up and be off,' the reporter whistled, snapping the band round his notebook. And Mrs Parker was stooping.

'I'm afraid I've dropped my glove. I'm so sorry to trouble you. Down there, between the seats . . .'

The gramophone was affirming in tones there was no denying, triumphant yet valedictory: *Dispersed are we; who have come together. But*, the gramophone asserted, *let us retain whatever made that harmony*.

O let us, the audience echoed (stooping, peering, fumbling), keep together. For there is joy, sweet joy, in company.

Dispersed are we, the gramophone repeated.

And the audience turning saw the flaming windows, each daubed with golden sun; and murmured: 'Home, gentlemen; sweet . . .' yet delayed a moment, seeing through the golden glory perhaps a crack in the boiler; perhaps a hole in the carpet; and hearing, perhaps, the daily drop of the daily bill.

Dispersed are we, the gramophone informed them. And dismissed them. So, straightening themselves for the last time, each grasping, it might be a hat, or a stick or a pair of suede gloves, for the last time they applauded Budge and Queen Bess; the trees; the white road; Bolney Minster; and the Folly. One hailed another, and they dispersed, across lawns, down paths, past the house to the gravel-strewn crescent, where cars, push bikes and cycles were crowded together.

Friends hailed each other in passing.

'I do think', someone was saying, 'Miss Whathername should have come forward and not left it to the rector . . . After all, she wrote it . . . I thought it brilliantly clever . . . O my dear, I thought it utter bosh. Did *you* understand the meaning? Well, he said she meant we all act all parts . . . He said, too, if I

caught his meaning, Nature takes part . . . Then there
was the idiot . . . Also, why leave out the Army, as
my husband was saying, if it's history? And if one
spirit animates the whole, what about the aeroplanes?
. . . Ah, but you're being too exacting. After all,
remember, it was only a village play . . . For my part,
I think they should have passed a vote of thanks to
the owners. When we had our pageant, the grass
didn't recover till autumn . . . Then we had tents . . .
That's the man, Cobbet of Cobbs Corner, who wins
all the prizes at all the shows. I don't myself admire
prize flowers, nor yet prize dogs . . .'

Dispersed are we, the gramophone triumphed, yet
lamented, *Dispersed are we* . . .

'But you must remember', the old cronies chatted,
'they had to do it on the cheap. You can't get people,
at this time o' year, to rehearse. There's the hay, let
alone the movies . . . What we need is a centre.
Something to bring us all together . . . The Brookes
have gone to Italy, in spite of everything. Rather
rash? . . . If the worst should come—let's hope it
won't—they'd hire an aeroplane, so they said . . .
What amused me was old Streatfield, feeling for his
pouch. I like a man to be natural, not always on a
perch . . . Then those voices from the bushes . . .
Oracles? You're referring to the Greeks? Were the
oracles, if I'm not being irreverent, a foretaste of our
own religion? Which is what? . . . Crepe soles? That's
so sensible . . . They last much longer and protect the

feet ... But I was saying: can the Christian faith
adapt itself? In times like these ... At Larting no one
goes to church ... There's the dogs, there's the
pictures ... It's odd that science, so they tell me, is
making things (so to speak) more spiritual ... The
very latest notion, so I'm told is, nothing's solid ...
There, you can get a glimpse of the church through
the trees ...

'Mr Umphelby! How nice to see you! Do come
and dine ... No, alas, we're going back to town. The
House is sitting ... I was telling them, the Brookes
have gone to Italy. They've seen the volcano. Most
impressive, so they say—they were lucky—in erup-
tion. I agree—things look worse than ever on the
continent. And what's the channel, come to think of
it, if they mean to invade us? The aeroplanes, I didn't
like to say it, made one think ... No, I thought it
much too scrappy. Take the idiot. Did she mean, so
to speak, something hidden, the unconscious as they
call it? But why always drag in sex ... It's true,
there's a sense in which we all, I admit, are savages
still. Those women with red nails. And dressing up—
what's that? The old savage, I suppose ... That's the
bell. Ding dong. Ding ... Rather a cracked old bell
... And the mirrors! Reflecting us ... I called that
cruel. One feels such a fool, caught unprotected ...
There's Mr Streatfield, going, I suppose to take the
evening service. He'll have to hurry, or he won't have
time to change ... He said she meant we all act. Yes,

but whose play? Ah, that's the question! And if we're left asking questions, isn't it a failure, as a play? I must say I like to feel sure if I go to the theatre, that I've grasped the meaning... Or was that, perhaps, what she meant?... Ding dong. Ding... that if we don't jump to conclusions, if you think, and I think, perhaps one day, thinking differently, we shall think the same?

'There's dear old Mr Carfax... Can't we give you a lift, if you don't mind playing bodkin?* We were asking questions, Mr Carfax, about the play. The looking-glasses now—did they mean the reflection is the dream; and the tune—was it Bach, Handel, or no one in particular—is the truth? Or was it t'other way about?

'Bless my soul, what a dither! Nobody seems to know one car from another. That's why I have a mascot, a monkey... But I can't see it... While we're waiting, tell me, did you feel when the shower fell, someone wept for us all? There's a poem, *Tears tears tears*,* it begins. And goes on O *then the unloosened ocean* ... but I can't remember the rest.

'Then when Mr Streatfield said: One spirit animates the whole—the aeroplanes interrupted. That's the worst of playing out of doors... Unless of course she meant that very thing... Dear me, the parking arrangements are not what you might call adequate ... I shouldn't have expected either so many His-pano-Suizas... That's a Rolls... That's a Bentley

... That's the new type of Ford ... To return to the meaning—Are machines the devil, or do they introduce a discord ... Ding dong, ding ... by means of which we reach the final ... Ding dong ... Here's the car with the monkey ... Hop in ... And goodbye, Mrs Parker ... Ring us up. Next time we're down don't forget ... Next time ... Next time ...'

The wheels scrurred on the gravel. The cars drove off.

The gramophone gurgled *Unity—Dispersity*. It gurgled *Un ... dis ...* And ceased.

The little company who had come together at luncheon were left standing on the terrace. The pilgrims had bruised a lane on the grass. Also, the lawn would need a deal of clearing up. Tomorrow the telephone would ring: 'Did I leave my handbag? ... A pair of spectacles in a red leather case? ... A little old brooch of no value to anyone but me?' Tomorrow the telephone would ring.

Now Mr Oliver said: 'Dear lady,' and, taking Mrs Manresa's gloved hand in his, pressed it, as if to say: 'You have given me what you now take from me.' He would have liked to hold on for a moment longer to the emeralds and rubies dug up, so people said, by thin Ralph Manresa in his ragamuffin days. But alas, sunset light was unsympathetic to her make-up; plated it looked, not deeply interfused. And he dropped her hand; and she gave him an arch roguish twinkle, as if to say—but the end of that sentence was cut short. For she turned, and Giles stepped forward; and the light breeze which the meteorologist had foretold fluttered her skirts; and she went, like a goddess, buoyant, abundant, with flower-chained captives following in her wake.

All were retreating, withdrawing and dispersing; and he was left with the ash grown cold and no glow, no glow on the log. What word expressed the sag at his heart, the effusion in his veins, as the retreating Manresa, with Giles attendant, admirable woman, all sensation, ripped the rag doll and let the sawdust stream from his heart?

The old man made a guttural sound, and turned to the right. On with the hobble, on with the limp, since the dance was over. He strolled alone past the trees. It was here, early that very morning, that he had destroyed the little boy's world. He had popped out with his newspaper; the child had cried.

Down in the dell, past the lily pool, the actors were undressing. He could see them among the brambles. In vests and trousers; unhooking; buttoning up: on all fours; stuffing clothes into cheap attaché cases; with silver swords, beards and emeralds on the grass. Miss La Trobe in coat and skirt—too short, for her legs were stout—battled with the billows of a crinoline. He must respect the conventions. So he stopped, by the pool. The water was opaque over the mud.

Then, coming up behind him, 'Oughtn't we to thank her?' Lucy asked him. She gave him a light pat on the arm.

How imperceptive her religion made her! The fumes of that incense obscured the human heart. Skimming the surface, she ignored the battle in the mud. After La Trobe had been excruciated by the Rector's interpretation, by the maulings and the manglings of the actors . . . 'She don't want our thanks, Lucy,' he said gruffly. What she wanted, like that carp (something moved in the water) was darkness in the mud; a whisky and soda at the pub; and coarse words descending like maggots through the waters.

'Thank the actors, not the author,' he said. 'Or ourselves, the audience.'

He looked over his shoulder. The old lady, the indigenous, the prehistoric, was being wheeled away by a footman. He rolled her through the arch. Now the lawn was empty. The line of the roof, the upright chimneys, rose hard and red against the blue of the evening. The house emerged; the house that had been obliterated. He was damned glad it was over—the scurry and the scuffle, the rouge and the rings. He stooped and raised a peony that had shed its petals. Solitude had come again. And reason and the lamplit paper . . . But where was his dog? Chained in a kennel? The little veins swelled with rage on his temples. He whistled. And here, released by Candish, racing across the lawn with a fleck of foam on the nostril, came his dog.

Lucy still gazed at the lily pool. 'All gone,' she murmured, 'under the leaves.' Scared by shadows passing, the fish had withdrawn. She gazed at the water. Perfunctorily she caressed her cross. But her eyes went water searching, looking for fish. The lilies were shutting; the red lily, the white lily, each on its plate of leaf. Above, the air rushed; beneath was water. She stood between two fluidities, caressing her cross. Faith required hours of kneeling in the early morning. Often the delight of the roaming eye seduced her—a sunbeam, a shadow. Now the jagged leaf at the corner suggested, by its contours, Europe. There were other leaves. She fluttered her eye over the surface, naming leaves India, Africa, America. Islands of security, glossy and thick.

'Bart . . .' She spoke to him. She had meant to ask him about the dragon-fly—couldn't the blue thread settle, if we destroyed it here, then there? But he had gone into the house.

Then something moved in the water; her favourite fantail. The golden orfe followed. Then she had a glimpse of silver—the great carp himself, who came to the surface so very seldom. They slid on, in and out between the stalks, silver; pink; gold; splashed; streaked; pied.

'Ourselves,' she murmured. And retrieving some glint of faith from the grey waters, hopefully, without much help from reason, she followed the fish; the speckled, streaked, and blotched; seeing in that vision beauty, power, and glory in ourselves.

Fish had faith, she reasoned. They trust us because we've never caught 'em. But her brother would reply: 'That's greed.' 'Their beauty!' she protested. 'Sex,' he would say. 'Who makes sex susceptible to beauty?' she would argue. He shrugged who? Why? Silenced, she returned to her private vision; of beauty which is goodness; the sea on which we float. Mostly impervious, but surely every boat sometimes leaks?

He would carry the torch of reason till it went out in the darkness of the cave. For herself, every morning, kneeling, she protected her vision. Every night she opened the window and looked at leaves against the sky. Then slept. Then the random ribbons of birds' voices woke her.

The fish had come to the surface. She had nothing to give them—not a crumb of bread. 'Wait, my darlings,' she addressed them. She would trot into the house and ask Mrs Sands for a biscuit. Then a shadow fell. Off they flashed. How vexatious! Who was it? Dear me, the young man whose name she had forgotten, not Jones; nor Hodge . . .

Dodge had left Mrs Manresa abruptly. All over the garden he had been searching for Mrs Swithin. Now he found her; and she had forgotten his name.

'I'm William,' he said. At that she revived, like a

girl in a garden in white among roses, who came running to meet him—an unacted part.

'I was going to get a biscuit—no, to thank the actors,' she stumbled, virginal, blushing. Then she remembered her brother. 'My brother', she added 'says one mustn't thank the author Miss La Trobe.'

It was always 'my brother . . . my brother' who rose from the depths of her lily pool.

As for the actors, Hammond had detached his whiskers and was now buttoning up his coat. When the chain was inserted between the buttons he was off.

Only Miss La Trobe remained, bending over something in the grass.

'The play's over,' he said. 'The actors have departed.'

'And we mustn't, my brother says, thank the author,' Mrs Swithin repeated, looking in the direction of Miss La Trobe.

'So I thank you,' he said. He took her hand and pressed it. Putting one thing with another, it was unlikely that they would ever meet again.

The church bells always stopped, leaving you to ask: Won't there be another note? Isa, half-way across the lawn, listened . . . Ding, dong, ding . . . There was not going to be another note. The congregation was assembled, on their knees, in the church. The service was beginning. The play was over; swallows skimmed the grass that had been the stage.

There was Dodge, the lip reader, her semblable,* her conspirator, a seeker like her after hidden faces. He was hurrying to rejoin Mrs Manresa who had gone in front with Giles—'the father of my children,' she muttered. The flesh poured over her, the hot, nerve wired, now lit up, now dark as the grave physical body. By way of healing the rusty fester of the poisoned dart she sought the face that all day long she had been seeking. Preening and peering, between backs, over shoulders, she had sought the man in grey. He had given her a cup of tea at a tennis party; handed her once, a racquet. That was all. But, she was crying, had we met before the salmon leapt like a bar of silver . . . had we met, she was crying. And when her little boy came battling through the bodies in the Barn 'Had he been his son,' she had muttered . . . In passing she stripped the bitter leaf that grew, as it happened, outside the nursery window. Old Man's Beard. Shrivelling the shreds in lieu of words, for no words grow there, nor roses either, she swept past her conspirator, her semblable, the seeker after vanished faces 'like Venus' he thought, making a rough translation, 'to her prey . . .'* and followed after.

Turning the corner, there was Giles attached to Mrs Manresa. She was standing at the door of her car. Giles had his foot on the edge of the running board. Did they perceive the arrows about to strike them?

[187]

'Jump in, Bill,' Mrs Manresa chaffed him.

And the wheels scurred on the gravel, and the car drove off.

At last, Miss La Trobe could raise herself from her stooping position. It had been prolonged to avoid attention. The bells had stopped; the audience had gone; also the actors. She could straighten her back. She could open her arms. She could say to the world, You have taken my gift! Glory possessed her—for one moment. But what had she given? A cloud that melted into the other clouds on the horizon. It was in the giving that the triumph was. And the triumph faded. Her gift meant nothing. If they had understood her meaning; if they had known their parts; if the pearls had been real and the funds illimitable—it would have been a better gift. Now it had gone to join the others.

'A failure,' she groaned, and stooped to put away the records.

Then suddenly the starlings attacked the tree behind which she had hidden. In one flock they pelted it like so many winged stones. The whole tree hummed with the whizz they made, as if each bird plucked a wire. A whizz, a buzz rose from the bird-buzzing, bird-vibrant, bird-blackened tree. The tree became a rhapsody, a quivering cacophony, a whizz and vibrant rapture, branches, leaves, birds syllabling discordantly life, life, life, without measure, without stop devouring the tree. Then up! Then off!

What interrupted? It was old Mrs Chalmers, creeping through the grass with a bunch of flowers—pinks apparently—to fill the vase that stood on her husband's grave. In winter it was holly, or ivy. In summer, a flower. It was she who had scared the starlings. Now she passed.

Miss La Trobe nicked the lock and hoisted the heavy case of gramophone records to her shoulder. She crossed the terrace and stopped by the tree where the starlings had gathered. It was here that she had suffered triumph, humiliation, ecstasy, despair—for nothing. Her heels had ground a hole in the grass.

It was growing dark. Since there were no clouds to trouble the sky, the blue was bluer, the green greener. There was no longer a view—no Folly, no spire of Bolney Minster. It was land merely, no land in particular. She put down her case and stood looking at the land. Then something rose to the surface.

'I should group them', she murmured, 'here.' It would be midnight; there would be two figures, half concealed by a rock. The curtain would rise. What would the first words be? The words escaped her.

Again she lifted the heavy suitcase to her shoulder. She strode off across the lawn. The house was dormant; one thread of smoke thickened against the trees. It was strange that the earth, with all those flowers incandescent—the lilies, the roses, and clumps of white flowers and bushes of burning green—should still be hard. From the earth green waters seemed to rise over her. She took her voyage away from the shore, and, raising her hand, fumbled for the latch of the iron entrance gate.

She would drop her suitcase in at the kitchen window, and then go on up to the Inn. Since the row with the actress who had shared her bed and her purse the need of drink had grown on her. And the horror and the terror of being alone. One of these days she would break—which of the village laws? Sobriety? Chastity? Or take something that did not properly belong to her?

At the corner she ran into old Mrs Chalmers returning from the grave. The old woman looked down at the dead flowers she was carrying and cut her. The women in the cottages with the red geraniums always did that. She was an outcast. Nature had somehow set her apart from her kind. Yet she had scribbled in the margin of her manuscript: 'I am the slave of my audience.'

She thrust her suitcase in at the scullery window and walked on, till at the corner she saw the red curtain at the bar window. There would be shelter; voices; oblivion. She turned the handle of the public house door. The acrid smell of stale beer saluted her; and voices talking. They stopped. They had been talking about Bossy as they called her—it didn't matter. She took her chair and looked through the

smoke at a crude glass painting of a cow in a stable;
also at a cock and a hen. She raised her glass to her
lips. And drank. And listened. Words of one syllable
sank down into the mud. She drowsed; she nodded.
The mud became fertile. Words rose above the intol-
erably laden dumb oxen plodding through the mud.
Words without meaning—wonderful words.

The cheap clock ticked; smoke obscured the picture. Smoke became tart on the roof of her mouth.
Smoke obscured the earth-coloured jackets. She no
longer saw them, yet they upheld her, sitting arms
akimbo with her glass before her. There was the high
ground at midnight; there the rock; and two scarcely
perceptible figures. Suddenly the tree was pelted with
starlings. She set down her glass. She heard the first
words.

Down in the hollow, at Pointz Hall, beneath the
trees, the table was cleared in the dining room.
Candish, with his curved brush had swept the
crumbs; had spared the petals and finally left the
family to dessert. The play was over, the strangers
gone, and they were alone—the family.

Still the play hung in the sky of the mind—moving,
diminishing, but still there. Dipping her raspberry in
sugar, Mrs Swithin looked at the play. She said,
popping the berry into her mouth, 'What did it

mean?' and added: 'The peasants; the kings; the fool and' (she swallowed) ourselves?'

They all looked at the play; Isa, Giles and Mr Oliver. Each of course saw something different. In another moment it would be beneath the horizon, gone to join the other plays. Mr Oliver, holding out his cheroot said: 'Too ambitious.' And, lighting his cheroot he added: 'Considering her means.'

It was drifting away to join the other clouds: becoming invisible. Through the smoke Isa saw not the play but the audience dispersing. Some drove; others cycled. A gate swung open. A car swept up the drive to the red villa in the cornfields. Low hanging boughs of acacia brushed the roof. Acacia petalled the car arrived.

'The looking-glasses and the voices in the bushes,' she murmured. 'What did she mean?'

'When Mr Streatfield asked her to explain, she wouldn't,' said Mrs Swithin.

Here, with its sheaf sliced in four, exposing a white cone, Giles offered his wife a banana. She refused it. He stubbed his match on the plate. Out it went with a little fizz in the raspberry juice.

'We should be thankful', said Mrs Swithin, folding her napkin, 'for the weather, which was perfect, save for one shower.'

Here she rose. Isa followed her across the hall to the big room.

They never pulled the curtains till it was too dark

to see, nor shut the windows till it was too cold. Why shut out the day before it was over? The flowers were still bright; the birds chirped. You could see more in the evening often when nothing interrupted, when there was no fish to order, no telephone to answer. Mrs Swithin stopped by the great picture of Venice—school of Canaletto.* Possibly in the hood of the gondola there was a little figure—a woman, veiled; or a man?

Isa, sweeping her sewing from the table, sank, her knee doubled, into the chair by the window. Within the shell of the room she overlooked the summer night. Lucy returned from her voyage into the picture and stood silent. The sun made each pane of her glasses shine red. Silver sparkled on her black shawl. For a moment she looked like a tragic figure from another play.

Then she spoke in her usual voice. 'We made more this year than last, he said. But then last year it rained.'

'This year, last year, next year, never—' Isa murmured. Her hand burnt in the sun on the window sill. Mrs Swithin took her knitting from the table.

'Did you feel', she asked 'what he said: we act different parts but are the same?'

'Yes,' Isa answered. 'No,' she added. It was Yes, No. Yes, yes, yes, the tide rushed out embracing. No, no, no, it contracted. The old boot appeared on the shingle.

[193]

'Orts, scraps and fragments,' she quoted what she remembered of the vanishing play.

Lucy had just opened her lips to reply, and had laid her hand on her cross caressingly, when the gentlemen came in. She made her little chirruping sound of welcome. She shuffled her feet to clear a space. But in fact there was more space than was needed, and great hooded chairs.

They sat down, ennobled both of them by the setting sun. Both had changed. Giles now wore the black coat and white tie of the professional classes, which needed—Isa looked down at his feet—patent leather pumps. 'Our representative, our spokesman,' she sneered. Yet he was extraordinarily handsome. 'The father of my children, whom I love and hate.' Love and hate—how they tore her asunder! Surely it was time someone invented a new plot, or that the author came out from the bushes . . .

Here Candish came in. He brought the second post on a silver salver. There were letters; bills; and the morning paper—the paper that obliterated the day before. Like a fish rising to a crumb of biscuit, Bartholomew snapped at the paper. Giles slit the flap of an apparently business document. Lucy read a criss-cross* from an old friend at Scarborough. Isa had only bills.

The usual sounds reverberated through the shell; Sands making up the fire; Candish stoking the boiler. Isa had done with her bills. Sitting in the shell of the room she watched the pageant fade. The flowers flashed before they faded. She watched them flash.

The paper crackled. The second hand jerked on. M. Daladier had pegged down the franc. The girl had gone skylarking with the troopers. She had screamed. She had hit him . . . What then?

When Isa looked at the flowers again, the flowers had faded.

Bartholomew flicked on the reading lamp. The circle of the readers, attached to white papers, was lit up. There in that hollow of the sun-baked field were congregated the grasshopper, the ant, and the beetle, rolling pebbles of sun-baked earth through the glistening stubble. In that rosy corner of the sun-baked field Bartholomew, Giles and Lucy polished and nibbled and broke off crumbs. Isa watched them.

Then the newspaper dropped.

'Finished?' said Giles, taking it from his father.

The old man relinquished his paper. He basked. One hand caressing the dog rippled folds of skin towards the collar.

The clock ticked. The house gave little cracks as if it were very brittle, very dry. Isa's hand on the window felt suddenly cold. Shadow had obliterated the garden. Roses had withdrawn for the night.

Mrs Swithin folding her letter murmured to Isa: 'I looked in and saw the babies, sound asleep, under the paper roses.'

'Left over from the coronation,' Bartholomew muttered, half asleep.

'But we needn't have been to all that trouble with the decorations,' Lucy added, 'for it didn't rain this year.'

'This year, last year, next year, never,' Isa murmured.

'Tinker, tailor, soldier, sailor,' Bartholomew echoed. He was talking in his sleep.

Lucy slipped her letter into its envelope. It was time to read now, her *Outline of History*. But she had lost her place. She turned the pages looking at pictures—mammoths, mastodons, prehistoric birds. Then she found the page where she had stopped.

The darkness increased. The breeze swept round the room. With a little shiver Mrs Swithin drew her sequin shawl about her shoulders. She was too deep in the story to ask for the window to be shut. 'England', she was reading, 'was then a swamp. Thick forests covered the land. On the top of their matted branches birds sang . . .'

The great square of the open window showed only sky now. It was drained of light, severe, stone cold. Shadows fell. Shadows crept over Bartholomew's high forehead; over his great nose. He looked leafless, spectral, and his chair monumental. As a dog shudders its skin, his skin shuddered. He rose, shook himself, glared at nothing, and stalked from the room.

They heard the dog's paws padding on the carpet behind him.

Lucy turned the page, quickly, guiltily like a child who will be told to go to bed before the end of the chapter.

'Prehistoric man,' she read, 'half-human, half-ape, roused himself from his semi-crouching position and raised great stones.'

She slipped the letter from Scarborough between the pages to mark the end of the chapter, rose, smiled, and tiptoed silently out of the room.

The old people had gone up to bed. Giles crumpled the newspaper and turned out the light. Left alone together for the first time that day, they were silent. Alone, enmity was bared; also love. Before they slept, they must fight; after they had fought, they would embrace. From that embrace another life might be born. But first they must fight, as the dog fox fights with the vixen, in the heart of darkness,* in the fields of night.

Isa let her sewing drop. The great hooded chairs had become enormous. And Giles too. And Isa too against the window. The window was all sky without colour. The house had lost its shelter. It was night before roads were made, or houses. It was the night that dwellers in caves had watched from some high place among rocks.

Then the curtain rose. They spoke.

[197]

EXPLANATORY NOTES

3 *Liskeard*: a town in Cornwall.

4 *tea-caddy locked*: tea, which bore a 112% tax in the eighteenth century, was worth locking up.

7 *the gardens*: Kensington Gardens in south-west central London; Kew Botanical Gardens on the Thames to the west of the city.

Hastings: seaside resort on the south coast.

8 *Outline of History*: a bestseller by H. G. Wells (1920).

12 *M. Daladier*: socialist politician, Prime Minister of France, 1838–40.

14 *Croydon*: London's pre-war airport.

15 *O'Neils*: approximately the name of the ancient Irish kings, from whom some later O'Neils claim descent.

18 *The Faerie Queene*: by Edmund Spenser (1596).

Kinglake's Crimea: A. W. Kinglake's *Invasion of the Crimea* (1863–87).

Kreutzer Sonata: by Tolstoy (1889).

Garibaldi: Giuseppe Garibaldi (1807–82), Italian statesman and soldier; in 1880 he proclaimed Victor Emmanuel King of Italy.

Palmerston: Henry John Temple, Viscount Palmerston (1784–1865), Liberal statesman, Prime Minister, 1855–8.

Eddington: Sir Arthur Eddington (1882–1944), astrophysicist and scientific popularizer.

Jeans: Sir James Jeans (1877–1946), physicist, astronomer, and author of popular books on science.

Whitehall: The headquarters of the Horse Guards are entered from this street, a centre of government.

22 *Antaeus*: giant son of Poseidon (Neptune); a wrestler credited with this method of recruiting his strength after a fall.

23 *Lemprière*: John Lemprière (d. 1824), author of a standard and much revised dictionary of classical mythology.

24 *the Coronation*: of George VI in 1937.

28 *Saints*: of St Swithin (d. 862) tradition holds that the weather on this day (15 July) will continue for forty more days.

29 *Bickley . . . Pyeminster*: like other place names in the book, these are invented for the occasion; one or two of them do actually occur, but in widely separated places.

Domesday Book: the record of William the Conqueror's land survey in 1086.

35 *Somerset House*: repository of wills and other documents.

37 *corkscrew*: it has been pointed out that champagne bottles are not opened by corkscrews; VW liked champagne and must have known this; was it required simply to cut the foil?

43 *sixteen men*: obscure; presumably the reference is to the Low Countries, but it is not clear what Giles read in his newspaper.

45 *Sir Joshua*: Sir Joshua Reynolds (1723–92), most famous of eighteenth-century portrait-painters.

48 *Figgis's Guide Book*: apparently an invention.

50 *'Fade far away . . . the fret'*: Keats, 'Ode to a Nightingale' (misquoted).

Constable: John Constable (1776–1837), landscape-painter.

Crome: John Crome (1768–1821), landscape-painter, called 'Old Crome' to distinguish him from his son John, also a painter.

54 *Gammer Gurton's Needle*: a play of uncertain authorship, perhaps by John Still, dated about 1553 and thought of as the first (or second) English comedy.

65 *Maples*: a famous furniture store in Tottenham Court Road, London.

69 Adsum: 'I am present' (used at roll call in some English schools).

76 Hawkins, Frobisher, Drake: Sir John Hawkins (1532–95), a naval commander; Sir Martin Frobisher (1535?–94), navigator; Sir Francis Drake (1540?–96), circumnavigator and naval commander.

78 *I fear I am not in my perfect mind*: *King Lear*, IV. vii. 62.

80 *the Globe theatre*: used by Shakespeare's company from 1598, and situated on the south bank of the Thames at Southwark.

83 Call for the robin ... wren: John Webster (1580?–1625?), *The White Devil*, v. iv. 100.

85 *skimble-skamble stuff*: *I Henry IV*, III. i. 153.

94 *King and Queen*: in 1939 they visited not India but Canada and the United States.

Duke of Windsor: Edward VIII (1894–1972) abdicated in 1936 and was made Duke of Windsor; Queen Mary, widow of George V, was his mother, famous as a hard bargainer for antique furniture.

98 *Windsor chair*: wooden chair with a back consisting of upright rods, with a cross-piece to hold them together.

104 'O sister swallow ... spring': A. C. Swinburne (1837–1909), *Itylus* (1864) (misquoted).

'Condemned in life's infernal mine ... pine ...': Samuel Johnson, 'On the Death of Dr Robert Levet' (misquoted).

Wellington: 1st Duke of Wellington (1769–1852), victor of Waterloo and later Prime Minister.

105 'Hark, hark, the dogs do bark ... town ...': nursery rhyme.

114 pounce-box: or 'pouncet-box'—small box with a perforated lid for perfume; used by Shakespeare and revived, according to *OED*, by Sir Walter Scott.

patch: a piece of black silk stuck on the face to show off the complexion.

Aqua Vitae: a distilled liquor such as brandy.

119 Peckham: London district south of the Thames, on the other side of the river from St Paul's, and a good way off.

122 the Mall: ceremonial avenue between Whitehall and Buckingham Palace.

125 Clytemnestra: wife of Greek leader Agamemnon; see Aeschylus' tragedy *Agamemnon*.

127 *Racine*: Jean Racine (1639–99), French classical dramatist.

Sandhurst: the military academy.

128 Gretna Green: eloping couples fled there to take advantage of the more permissive Scottish marriage law.

130 messuages; tenements: legal terms: roughly, dwelling houses and the land associated with them.

131 chalk stones: white deposits in the hands and feet, associated with gout.

132 off with the raggle-taggle gipsies: nursery song.

134 *Ascot*: the race-meeting there in June is always an occasion for women to display their finery, especially their hats.

136 *Gladstone*: W. E. Gladstone (1809–98), Prime Minister four times between 1868 and 1894.

142 *hansom ... growler*: the hansom was a two-wheeled, the growler a four-wheeled cab.

Seven Dials: London district notorious in the nineteenth century as a haunt of criminals.

Garotters: criminals who strangled their victims (apparently a not uncommon form of assault in nineteenth-century London).

Regent Street. Piccadilly. Hyde Park Corner ... Covent Garden: central London districts.

the old Duke: the Duke of Wellington (see note to p. 104).

the Park: Hyde Park.

Old Kent Road: in the East End of London.

142–3 *Crystal Palace*: a glass structure erected in Hyde Park for the Great Exhibition (1851) and subsequently moved to a south London site, where it was later destroyed by fire.

144 *Parliament Square*: outside the Houses of Parliament.

145 Mansion House: the official residence of the Lord Mayor of London in the City.

Ireland; Famine. Fenians: the Irish famine of the 1840s; the Irish Republican Brotherhood, founded 1857.

146 Cripplegate; St Giles; Whitechapel; the Minories: poor districts of east- and west-central London.

the Abbey: Westminster Abbey.

152 'The Last Rose of Summer': from the *Irish Melodies* (1807) of Thomas Moore (1779–1852).

'I never loved a Dear Gazelle': from Moore's *Lalla Rookh* (1817).

155 mechanics' institute: educational establishment for working men.

157 *'Shakespeare and the musical glasses'*: quoted from Chapter 9 of Oliver Goldsmith's *The Vicar of Wakefield* (1766).

163 *the League of . . .* : the League of Nations, founded 1919, dissolved 1946.

164 *temple-haunting martins*: 'temple-haunting martlets', Shakespeare, *Macbeth*, I. vi. 4.

in the crannied wall: Tennyson, 'Flower in the crannied wall'.

166 I am not . . . in my perfect mind: see note to p. 78.

Home is the hunter: R. L. Stevenson (1850–94), 'Requiem'.

Sweet and low: Tennyson, *The Princess*.

Is that a dagger: *Macbeth*, II. i. 33 (misquoted).

In thy will is our peace: 'E' n la sua voluntade è nostra pace', Dante, *Paradiso*, iii. 85.

172 *treading, like angels*: 'For fools rush in where angels fear to tread', Alexander Pope, *Essay on Criticism*, e. 625 (1711).

[202]

EXPLANATORY NOTES

180 *playing bodkin*: 'to ride bodkin' is to be wedged between two other passengers (cf. Thackeray, *Vanity Fair*, ch. 40).

Tears, tears, tears: unexplained.

187 *her semblable*: referring to a line by Charles Baudelaire: 'Hypocrite lecteur, mon semblable, mon frère', used by VW's friend T. S. Eliot in *The Waste Land*.

'like Venus . . . to her prey . . .': 'C'est Vénus tout entière à sa proie attacheé', Racine, *Phèdre*, Act I, Scene iii.

193 *Canaletto*: Giovanni Antonio Canal (1697–1768), painter of Venice and London.

194 *a criss-cross*: until well into the nineteenth century postage, charged to the recipient by the sheet, was expensive, so to save stamp duty the letter-writer often continued diagonally across a page already filled in the usual way; the practice was of course long obsolete by 1939.

197 *heart of darkness*: pan-allusion, presumably deliberate, to the title of Conrad's short novel.

*The
Oxford
World's
Classics
Website*

www.worldsclassics.co.uk

- Browse the full range of Oxford World's Classics online

- Sign up for our monthly e-alert to receive information on new titles

- Read extracts from the Introductions

- Listen to our editors and translators talk about the world's greatest literature with our Oxford World's Classics audio guides

- Join the conversation, follow us on Twitter at OWC_Oxford

- Teachers and lecturers can order inspection copies quickly and simply via our website

www.worldsclassics.co.uk

American Literature

British and Irish Literature

Children's Literature

Classics and Ancient Literature

Colonial Literature

Eastern Literature

European Literature

Gothic Literature

History

Medieval Literature

Oxford English Drama

Poetry

Philosophy

Politics

Religion

The Oxford Shakespeare

A complete list of Oxford World's Classics, including Authors in Context, Oxford English Drama, and the Oxford Shakespeare, is available in the UK from the Marketing Services Department, Oxford University Press, Great Clarendon Street, Oxford OX2 6DP, or visit the website at www.oup.com/uk/worldsclassics.

In the USA, visit www.oup.com/us/owc for a complete title list.

Oxford World's Classics are available from all good bookshops. In case of difficulty, customers in the UK should contact Oxford University Press Bookshop, 116 High Street, Oxford OX1 4BR.

D. H. LAWRENCE	**The Rainbow**
	Sons and Lovers
	The White Peacock
	Women in Love
	The Widowing of Mrs Holroyd and Other Plays
KATHERINE MANSFIELD	**Selected Stories**
VIRGINIA WOOLF	**Between the Acts**
	Flush
	Jacob's Room
	Mrs Dalloway
	Night and Day
	Orlando: A Biography
	A Room of One's Own and Three Guineas
	To the Lighthouse
	The Voyage Out
	The Waves
	The Years
W. B. YEATS	**The Major Works**